uv⁰

35 –

RATS IN THE TREES

Rats in the Trees

Stories by Jess Mowry

John Daniel and Company, Publishers
Santa Barbara, CA · 1990

To Howard Junker,
for promising nothing but a lot of hard work.
And for Victor—go for it, brother.

"One Way" was first published in *ZYZZYVA*. "The Ship" was first published in *Sequoia*. "Perv" was first published in *Alchemy*.

Cover photography by Channing Bates
Design and typography by Jim Cook/Santa Barbara.

LIBRARY OF CONGRESS CATALOGING-IN-PUBLICATION DATA

Mowry, Jess, 1960–
    Rats in the trees: stories / Jess Mowry.
        p. cm.
    Summary: Arriving in Oakland with his skateboard and
dreams of living by the ocean, thirteen-year-old Robby befriends
the Animals, a street gang whose culture is based on skateboards,
beer, rap slang, and danger.
    ISBN 0-936784-81-4: $8.95
    [1. Gangs—Fiction. 2. California—Fiction. 3. Afro-Ameri-
cans—Fiction.] I. Title.
PZ7.M86655Rat   1990   89-27909
[Fic]—dc20   CIP AC

Published by John Daniel & Company, Publishers
Post Office Box 21922, Santa Barbara, California 93121

Distributed by Texas Monthly Press
Post Office Box 1569, Austin, Texas 78767

Rats in the Trees:

Welcome to Oakland

*R*OBBY *twisted in the seat, his nose pressed to hot glass, and watched as the other Greyhound pulled away. He still might've made it, grabbing for the paper bag and skateboard beside him, but it just didn't seem worth the hassle somehow. Fuck it. He was tired. He slumped back with a sigh, tears burning his eyes. He fought them, sight blurring as he looked down the bus's empty length to a big black number above the windshield.*

Wrong bus, lame-o, he thought. No wonder he'd sat here for so long and nobody else had gotten on.

His stomach was empty and tight with that scared feeling he remembered from when he'd tried to skate down the bridge shoulder. He'd lost it halfway, ending a bloody mess in weeds and gravel, but hadn't cried. For sure he'd wanted to, but Jeffers, Ted, and Ryan were watching.

He dug in his pocket for the ticket; FRESNO, CA to SAN FRAN-CISCO, CA, it read. ONE WAY. Outside, faded letters on cinder block said, WELCOME TO OAKLAND. It was hot in the empty bus, and

7

strangely quiet after hearing the engine drone all those hours. He listened as other busses came and went and people talked and laughed. There were a few kid-voices, happy with someone to meet them. Sweat trickled from under Robby's bushy hair and his black Steadham T-shirt stuck to his chest. He pulled up his legs and huddled in the seat. Jeffers kept ragging him that his hair looked like an old-fashioned Afro, but Robby liked it that way. Thinking of Jeffers and the other dudes brought that crying feeling again, but he held it back and hugged his knees. There was no time for that kind of kid stuff now.

He jammed the ticket into his pocket, checking that the sweat-wet five-dollar bill was still there, and forced himself to think. Jeez, turd-brain, he told himself, there had to be a zillion other busses going to San Francisco. So he'd missed this one? B.F.D. Nothing to get all hyper about. People missed busses all the time. Nobody cried over it. He glanced out the window again. What the hell did it matter anyway? Wasn't like he had to be somewhere on time anymore. He could do what he fucking well wanted.

Robby considered that. It was a strange feeling; a little lonely maybe, but better than when he'd heard he was getting stuck in a foster home. Ryan was in one of those, and they fed him rice and beans all the time, got him lame clothes at Goodwill, and broke his nose.

Jeez, it was hot! He'd thought anywhere they had ocean was going to be cool, like Jeffers had said. This was even worse than Fresno, with the diesel smoke, hot oil stink, and a strange stickiness in the air that made it hard to breathe. Dudes here had to skate in nothing but baggies or cutoffs, deadly on knees. Or maybe they all surfed?

Robby pictured a bunch of surf kids, blond, blue-eyed, and tanned almost to his own warm bronze. On TV there would always be one black kid with any group of whiteys, even if it didn't really seem to work that way. He frowned. These dudes would say different stuff—maybe "hot" for "cool" and "awesome" for "hot." A few wrong words and he'd look totally lame and no one would like him, even if he could shred to the max on his board. He picked up his board and held it tight—a killer Steve Steadham with Indy 169s, black Bullet wheels, and scarred Saber-Tooth ribs—definitely not a pose-plank.

He looked out the window once more and wondered how far San

Francisco was. At least you could feel like somebody on a bus. But Jeffers had said there was an ocean in Oakland too. What difference did it make? It was four in the afternoon and hotter than hell. He snagged his stuff and walked up the aisle.

A bus driver was walking past as Robby reached the door, a black dude who had his gray jacket slung over his shoulder like a street kid would.

"Um?" said Robby.

The driver stopped. He looked tired and hot and not too stoked. "Yeah?"

"Um, I think I missed the San Francisco bus."

The driver glanced down at Robby—sweaty clothes that'd been slept in, ragged jeans with one knee gone, T-shirt too big, and worn-out Pumas. There was the usual brown bag, falling apart, and his best possession, the skateboard. The kid might as well have been wearing a sign. The driver sighed. He'd seen all these kids before and mostly wished he hadn't. It didn't matter what color, and they got younger every year. Something was wrong somewhere and getting worse all the time. The driver had kids, and one had a board. This boy was sort of chubby and cute, but there was muscle under the padding and that city hardness in those wary brown eyes.

"Let's see your ticket, dude."

The driver squinted at it a moment, then handed it back. Another day in that sweaty pocket and nobody'd be able to read it anymore. "I think there's another bus in about an hour. Check with the counter inside." The driver hesitated a moment, but what the hell else could he do? "Hey, an' be careful with that ticket, dude, otherwise they run you outa here." He walked away.

One Way

ROBBY pushed open the station door, carrying his board by the front truck, downside in. At least it was cool inside. He smelled burgers from the restaurant and his stomach growled, but five and change wouldn't go far. Maybe he could live off his fat awhile like those bears on TV? He saw a whole cigarette under a chair and snagged it fast. Matches were always a prob, but Jeffers had given him his Bic and it was still half full.

He walked across to a black plastic TV-chair, just like the one in Fresno. He slid behind the little screen and pulled out his lighter, wondering if they had the Thundercats or Ninja Turtles here. It wasn't worth risking a quarter to find out. The cigarette was one of those pussy kind, so he broke off the filter before firing. The smoke eased his hunger a little, but that cleaning shit they used on the floor was giving him a headache.

A rattler in a baggy uniform came over. He was white and bored. He glanced at the cigarette, but seemed to figure there were better things to hassle about. "You got a ticket, kid?"

Robby dug it out. The rattler gave it a look, then flipped it back, jerking a thumb at the big clock over the doors. "Next one leaves at five-twenty, kid. Be on it." He smiled with his mouth. "And put a fucking quarter in or get outta the chair."

"Dipshit," came to Robby's mind. He took a big cool hit off the cigarette and blew smoke, watching the rattler's eyes narrow. Then he slid out of the chair and walked *the* walk toward the bathroom, feeling the rattler watching. "Lame-o," he whispered.

A tall skinny black boy stood by the door. They'd call him dribble-lips in Fresno. He looked about sixteen and also like he knew everything about Robby. "Crackers," he murmured. "A dollar."

Robby knew crackers, though they were called nukes in Fresno, and a dollar was way too much. He almost smiled. Like the TV said, "Just say no," asshole. He ignored the dude: scoring the right local word was worth the shove he got. He did smile then, hearing the rattler's squeaky cop-shoes cross the floor and the one word, *"Out!"*

"Yeah, right," the skinny dude yawned. Robby knew he'd be back.

The bathroom was all shiny tile under flickering fluorescents. It smelled like piss and Pine-Sol. There was a white dude, old, twenty-something, leaning on the line of sinks. He smiled at Robby.

Homo, Robby thought. Perv. Anybody who hung out where it smelled like piss had to be weird. Things weren't so different here. He saw the long trough and the dude watching him. He hated those things—out in the open, always too fucking high. How could anybody piss trying to stand on their toes? Everything else was a goddamn pay toilet except one and there was somebody in it. A fucking dime to piss! At least he could shut the door. He paid the box a dime and went in, sighing, yanking his zipper, and making as much water-noise as he could. He should've used the one right there on the bus; had to start figuring stuff like that.

He jerked up his zipper, flipped the cigarette in the toilet, and flushed. Then he laid the skateboard across the seat and sat, swinging his legs. Should he go for San Francisco? Trouble was, he didn't know how long that would take. It would probably be dark when he got there, too late for the ocean, and they'd run him off without a ticket. He'd slept on the street before, a few times when his folks were

11

fighting, a couple more with Jeffers and Tad when they'd scored some beer and gotten too wasted to skate or even walk. It'd be a lot easier to find some place behind a dumpster. . . .

Somebody tapped on the door. Robby saw the perv's Adidas underneath. "Hey, kid, want to play a game?"

Robby grinned. Games were shit old people thought up for kids. He'd never let a perv touch him before but Jamie had, in Rotting Park, and got $20. He'd said it was weird, but not bad. Jeffers said you could score a sixer that way, sometimes, but to get it first. Robby sat and kicked his legs. The door was locked, even if the perv put in another dime. What was he going to do, crawl under?

"How much?" Robby asked. That's what Jeffers would say.

The perv sounded like he had hurt feelings or something. "Hey, little guy, I just want to be your friend."

"Yeah right, duuude!" Suddenly Robby laughed and almost couldn't stop. It was *too* funny. A dime bought you a piss and a perv in Oakland. "Fuck-off, queer," he said.

The perv said nothing, but the Adidas didn't move.

"I'll scream," Robby added. "Loud."

The Adidas went away.

Sunlight slanted yellow in hot evening air as Robby pushed open the station door. He'd figured he might as well check the place out. There must be an ocean around somewhere. A black kid went by on a board, a thrasher old VariFlex. They ignored each other but checked boards; Robby's was better and they both knew it. The kid wore ragged jeans and had his shirt tied around his waist, hanging down in back. Robby pulled his off and did the same. The cracker dude was standing by a streetlamp, looking like he wanted to kick the shit out of somebody. Robby decked and rolled. It didn't matter which way, but he thought of the ocean again. Jeffers said you could sleep on the beach.

Wheels clicked cracks and the blocks passed. Robby stayed on a straight line to somewhere. These sidewalks were crowded, and he was too busy dodging people to pay much attention to anything else. The concrete was old and rough. The curbs were different too, but there was a lot of scraped skateboard paint on them.

The sun lowered and grew orange in distant fog. The air cooled and he stopped sweating. He passed another boy on a board, a little black dude on a Punk-Size. The kid didn't seem to figure there was anything special about Robby and that felt good and bad at the same time.

The food smells from the restaurants bothered him: there were so many. He tailed in front of a Doggie Diner and thought about a hot dog, but there was another cigarette under a bus bench and he snagged that instead, firing as he rolled. It didn't seem to help his hunger much and it buzzed his head a little. He pinched it halfway, dropping it in the bag for later.

The streets were quiet now, and he heard a car come around the far corner. He tensed a moment, glancing up the street—van, Dodge, dark blue, maybe black, it was getting hard to see as the daylight faded. He looked around but there was no place to hide. Was there any reason to? Heavy-metal music echoed between the buildings. Robby flipped up his board and pretended to be checking the trucks while watching the van from the corner of his eye as it neared. It didn't have its lights on but the driver must have seen him because it eased toward the curb. Robby almost decked, but the music faded low and a kid-voice called. "Yo, shredder!"

The van pulled over and stopped. The voice was friendly, breaking in the middle the way Jeffers' did sometimes. "Want some beer, brother?"

Robby came slowly to the open passenger window, ready to book fast. The kid inside was white, thin, with super-long bleached metaler hair. He wore black Levis, black Iron Maiden T-shirt, big studded collar, and a heavy spiked wrist-cuff. He also had on those expensive studded riot-gloves. Total showtime, Robby thought, no good for skating. But his blue eyes were friendly.

Robby leaned on the door, looking in. If the kid was old enough for a license, it was just. The dude grinned at Robby. Both his front teeth were those stainless-steel kind they sometimes put in kids until they were old enough for real fake ones.

Total metaler or what, flashed through Robby's mind. But at the same time he felt a little sorry for the dude—other kids probably called him tin-grin, or something. The dude held out an open can of Bud.

Robby took it, sipped, then chugged a decent hit. It was kid-beer, kind of flat and warm, but he was thirsty and warm beer kept you from being hungry.

"What's up, bro?" the dude asked.

Robby considered. "Um, just skatin' home, man."

Robby handed back the can and the dude nodded, chugging, not even wiping the top first. Robby stood on tiptoes, pressing closer to the door. The metal was still sun-warm and felt good.

"Yeah?" said the dude. "Figured you must live around here 'cause you've got a board. Um, what kind?"

Robby held it up. "Just a thrasher old Steadham. Nuthin' rad. You ride, man?"

The dude grinned again and passed back the Bud. "Not since I got my wheels!" He patted the dash. "Used to have a Roskopp."

"Yeah?" said Robby. "They're totally bad!"

"Where do you live? I could give you a ride if you want."

Robby's eyes flicked to the back of the van. Carpeted, paneled, but totally empty, nowhere anybody else could be hiding. "Um, by the beach."

Robby left a couple swallows in the can and passed it back. It wasn't cool to kill it. The dude gave Robby another metal grin and finished it. *"Beach?* Oh yeah. I guess it would be for you. Well, guess that means you're almost home anyway, don't it?" He studied Robby a minute. "Um, how old are you, man?"

"Thirteen."

"Naw. Hey, open the door a second, let me see ya."

Robby did, stepping back. The dude checked him and grinned. "No way, man! You're way too big for thirteen."

Robby smiled a little. At least he hadn't said fat.

"Hey!" said the dude. "I got one more Bud left. You wanna slide in an' we'll just sit here an' split it? You like Slayer?"

Robby considered. It was getting darker by the minute and the street was empty and dead. The van smelled good inside—like leather and kids, beer and smoke. The dome light had come on when the door opened. It was painted red and made the interior look warm. Maybe

14

with a half-Bud in his stomach he wouldn't be hungry tonight. Robby climbed in.

The dude pulled another Bud from between the seats and popped it, checking Robby again. "Hey, bro, no shit, you are big an' bad. I guess all you dudes are like that, huh?" He gave Robby firsts.

Robby frowned a little. "Um, what do you mean?"

"Aw, nothing." The kid smiled again. "Hey, I know how lame this's gonna sound, but my best friend is a black dude. I known him since third-grade. All you dudes are just naturally cool."

Robby sipped beer and smiled. "Or what."

The kid gave Robby another long look. For just a second, Robby wanted to cross his arms over his chest. "My little brother's thirteen too, only he's a total marshmallow compared to you. I guess all you bros have to be super bad to live here, huh? I mean, you know how to fight, an' carry guns an' everything?"

Robby thought a second. "Yeah."

"Full-autos, huh?"

"Sometimes." Robby passed back the Bud. The dude studied him a few moments. "Um, could I touch you, bro? I mean, I ain't no homo or nothing! I just can't believe you're only thirteen."

Robby tensed and slid close to the door. "Um, no, man. I know you're not a homo. I just don't wanna be touched, okay? I, um, gotta get home anyways. Thanks for the beer, bro." Robby slid out, watching the dude watching him. The kid started to reach for something between the seats, then gave Robby another grin.

"Hey. It's cool, bro! I don't blame you. We had those pervert movies in school too."

Robby stood on the sidewalk for a moment then closed the van's door. "It's okay, bro. I just gotta get home, that's all. My dad'll get pissed. Um, thanks again for the Bud . . . an' I think your van is totally bad."

He rolled a couple blocks more, then stopped and looked around. The buildings were old and dirty brick, faded like rust in the evening light. No more stores, only a little corner market. The rest were garages and body shops, all closed. The sidewalk was totally thrashed, broken and littered with bottles and trash. There was a wino in a doorway. It was so ugly and familiar and stupid that it made him homesick. But the salt smell was strong and he rolled on.

Parked trucks and abandoned cars lined the curbs. Windows at street level were barred or covered with plywood. He looked at the spray-painted words and pictures, some familiar—the Anarchy sign, Hip-Hop, good old FUCK YOU. But there weren't any squared-off Chicano letters and there was lots of heavy-metal and punker stuff and rap.

Robby jumped the gutter, cut the street, and slapped the opposite curb. A spray-paint design in red and black, like a Tiger-Dog snarling from a letter A, faced him from a corner wall—a gang-mark for sure. It was old, but nobody'd painted "sucks" or something underneath or an "anti" sign over it. Whatever the Tiger-Dog stood for, it got respect. It wasn't very high on the wall, he noticed, just about where he'd have painted it. For sure, there were kid-gangs in Fresno, but the big dudes always painted out their marks fast.

He rounded another corner and there it was. He tailed and stared and fought back tears. It sucked!

There was no surf. The water stretched away, silent and sullen. There was no beach. The water lapped at rotten pilings, broken rock, and rusty junk. No sand, only stinking black mud. Further up the shore, dim in a fog as gray and ugly as a tule fog in Fresno, was a short wharf alongside a crumbling warehouse.

Snagging his board, Robby walked over to a rusted chain-link gate. The wire on one corner was peeled back and he squeezed through. The wharf planking was rotten and gone in places. He walked to the end and sat, dangling his legs, looking down at dirty black water where garbage floated. He pulled out the half-cigarette and fired. Tears burned his eyes again, and this time he let them fall.

He should've figured it would be like this. The ocean was just as worn-out and thrashed as everything else in the whole fucking world! Things were no different anywhere; and, if there really were white sandy beaches and surf-kids, it would be a kind of mall-place with rattlers to keep him out. This was all the ocean he was ever going to get.

The last light faded and Robby sat alone in foggy darkness. He smoked until the cigarette burned his fingers. The fog was wet and cold and he put his shirt back on. He wished he had enough beer so he could drink until he couldn't see or feel anything anymore. Then he pulled up his knees, put his head between his legs, and cried.

Something creaked behind him, but he didn't look. He didn't care. Let the Tiger-Dogs come and beat the shit out of him; maybe they'd kill him. Maybe that was better.

There was breathing, the deep kind, like you make when you're drunk. Then, a kid-voice: "Whitey?"

That was funny. Even now. Robby turned, looking up at the fattest kid he'd ever seen.

For sure, a lot of Mexican kids were fat, but this dude was black. He looked about Robby's age, though it was hard to tell in the dark. He wore jeans that sagged under his belly, thrasher Nikes that used to be white, and a ragged black T-shirt with what looked like RATT on the front and couldn't cover his middle. The fat kid stopped a few feet away and checked Robby. "You ain't Whitey."

Robby shrugged. He couldn't see anybody else around and sure wasn't scared of this fat tub. "Duh."

That didn't seem to bother the fat kid. He smiled a little, funny, like he knew a secret or something and Robby wondered if he was a retard.

"Yeah? You ain't from here," the dude said.

"No shit."

"Yeah? So, where?"

"So nuthin'! I'm Panthro from Third-Earth, duuude!"

The fat kid only smiled wider and that bothered Robby.

"Yeah? I'm into the Thundercats too, man. You look more like one of Mum-ra's dipshits. Wanna get your ass wiped?"

"By *you*? I doubt!"

The fat kid grinned, teeth big and white. "Yeah? You in Animal-Land now, dude. Lion-o ain't gonna save your ass here."

Robby considered that and the fat kid moved a lot faster than it looked like he could, snagging Robby's board with a grunt. Robby jumped up, but the dude was checking his board like an expert, though he couldn't have ridden one for his life. Robby wanted to snatch it back and punch that huge belly, hard, but the dude handled the board with respect.

"Steadham," the fat kid said. He grinned even wider. "That's what Whitey rides too. Um, synchronicity, man!" He checked the downside, and pointed to a sticker. "Skully Brothers. I heard of them. They gots an ad in *Thrasher*. They in, um ... "

"Fresno."

"Yeah." The fat kid handed the board back, and Robby couldn't help it, he asked, "You, um, *ride,* man?"

The dude smiled, shy. "Naw. But the other Animals all shred to the max, 'specially Randers an' Kevin." He studied Robby a minute. "Whitey's pretty intense too. You sure look a lot like him."

Robby was used to white kids saying stupid stuff like that, but a black dude should know better. Anyway, "How the fuck could I look like a whitey, man?"

"Whitey's black, an' kinda fat too."

"I ain't fat! Not like you!"

The fat kid giggled. "Yeah? Now you even *sound* like Whitey!"

"Fuckin' A!"

"Nobody says *that* anymore."

"Then, why's he called Whitey?"

" 'Cause."

Robby thought a minute. There was an open doorway on the side of the warehouse and the other ... Animals ... were probably in there laughing. For sure, he was going to get beat up. He shrugged again. "What the fuck, man. I'm Robby. You got a smoke or you just gonna kick my ass? Go ahead. I don't give a shit!"

The fat kid gave him that funny smile again, then dug a squashed Marlboro hardpack from a pocket and straightened two cigarettes. They fired off Robby's Bic.

"I'm Donny," the fat kid said. "Randers might kick it." He considered. "Or maybe just do you best-moves-for-keeps an' score himself another board."

Robby didn't say anything. He'd lost his last board that way. He took a big hit off the Marlboro and it buzzed his head. He didn't care about that either. The other dudes would probably show in a minute anyway.

Donny sank down and dangled his legs. Robby checked the doorway again, then slowly sat alongside. They smoked and spat in the water. Donny smelled a little like burger grease and Robby's belly rumbled.

"So, where's Fresno?" Donny asked.

"A long ways."

"Yeah? How'd you get here? You don't got to say."

"On a lame-o bus."

"Yeah? How come? You don't got to say."

"I ran away, man."

Donny blew smoke. "Yeah? Kevin don't hardly go home no more either. He didn't run as far as you. Just used to get wasted all the time an' sleep in dumpsters."

"I done that."

"Yeah? Only now he stays at the Center a lot with Nathaniel."

"Who's Nathaniel? Some kinda social-worker lady?"

Donny spat. "Nathaniel is a *boy,* man! Kinda."

Robby told himself to be cool. He could blow it easy with stupid questions and these dudes would figure him a squid and kick his ass. "That, um, Tiger-Dog your mark? It's pretty hot."

"Yeah. I do 'em." Donny looked back at the water. "I figure that's why they let me be a Animal."

Mascot, Robby thought. That figured. But some gang mascots were pretty important. He knew better than to ask how many Animals there were . . . or *where* they were. "Must be some bad dudes?"

"Or what! Even the dealers leave us alone. Most of the time." Donny sat a little straighter. "We kicked the shit outta some old perv what beat up Kevin a few weeks ago! Sent him bawlin' back to Silicone-land, man!" He looked at Robby. "So, where you sleepin'? You don't got to say."

Robby shrugged and looked back at the doorway. He really didn't feel like getting beat up.

Donny smiled. "Like King Kong?"

"Huh?"

"Any fuckin' place he wants to?"

Robby looked down at the water and nodded.

Donny glanced over his shoulder at the doorway, then back at Robby. "I'm alone, man." He flipped his cigarette away and stretched. "You hungry?"

Robby nodded again.

"Yeah? Me too. C'mon. My mom don't get home till around ten an' we got lots of stuff. You stay out here, for sure you get your ass wiped. Randers is cool, but he got no time for strange dudes, an' Kevin, shit, man, you wouldn't want to meet Kevin in the dark!" Donny struggled to his feet. "Um, why was you cryin', man? You don't got to say."

Robby thought a minute, then shrugged and pointed. "Your ocean sucks."

Donny looked out over the Bay. The fog was too thick to see San Francisco or even the Bridge going across. He gave Robby another funny smile. "Yeah."

Donny led through the doorway into blackness. They came out the front, walked a couple of blocks back up from the water, and turned into a door, then up a narrow box-stairs that smelled like old piss. The steps ended at a hall. A dim bulb burned halfway down and more light filtered through a window from a streetlamp. It looked to Robby like the floor tilted. The boards squeaked and popped and there was a lot of stuff spray-painted on the walls. Donny went to the far end, dug two keys from a pocket, and undid the locks on a door that looked like somebody'd tried to kick down a couple times. The hinges were loose as Donny shoved it open. He flipped a switch and Robby got that homesick feeling again. Not much was different anywhere.

There was one room, half of it kitchen. The other half had some thrashed furniture and pictures of Martin Luther King and JFK on top of an old TV. There was a messy bed under the window, Donny's for sure. A half-open door showed a bathroom, and another door, closed, was probably his mom's room.

Donny pushed the hall door closed and snapped the locks. "Okay, huh?"

Robby nodded.

Donny pulled off his shirt and kicked out of his Nikes. "You like burgers, man?"

"Or what! Um, can I use your bathroom?"

"For sure. Um, pick up the seat or my mom has a cow." Donny snapped on the TV, then went to the fridge and started knocking stuff around inside. He held up a can of Budweiser as Robby came back. "Wanna beer, man?"

"For sure! Um, your mom *let* you drink beer?"

"Naw . . . leastways not at home. She seen me drunk on my ass a couple times an' had a cow. I got this sixer from Weasel today an' gotta do somethin' with it before she gets back. We can drink it if you wanna."

"Um, don't Weasel get pissed?"

"Naw. The Animals always gots beer."

Robby took the can and popped it, taking a small hit. He knew better than to chug on an empty stomach. "Um, you dudes do anything but beer, man?"

Donny squashed some gobs of hamburger on the counter and plopped them in a big black pan. "Beer mostly. For sure everybody's checked out all the other shit, but it's hard to ride on most of that stuff. Kevin still does some rock once in a while an' Rix an' Randers both did some dust a couple weeks ago." He dropped the pan on the stove. "They both blew it an' Nathaniel had to chill 'em out. Nathaniel don't like that kinda shit. He's cool an' don't say nuthin', but you can tell. What you do in Fresno, man?"

"Me an' my friend Jeffers did some nuke a couple of weeks ago."

"What?"

"Um, cracker?"

"Yeah? Intense, huh?"

"Aw, only for a little while. You got to keep doin' more. Shit's cheap but it still runs into bucks. I don't like to mega-think anyways. Scary sometimes." He looked at the Bud can. "Figure most of the shredders only do this stuff . . . maybe some doob once in a while."

"Yeah. That's about like it is here. What's Fresno like, man? You got mountains an' stuff?"

"Naw, Fresno got total zip, man! It sucks!"

Donny turned. "Yeah? Didn't you see nuthin' nice comin' on the bus?"

"It was at night, mostly. Then today I was sleepin'. Ain't nuthin' nice nowhere, man."

"Yeah."

Robby looked at the TV. It was an old Silver Spoons rerun. Ricky was all bummed-out and crying because his dad wouldn't get him a new video game. Robby sipped beer. Behind him, Donny said, "*That* dude's got some nice shit."

"Yeah. But he's still got probs, man. He's got all that stuff an' still gots probs. I never seen him just hangin' with his friends, y'know? Just hangin' out somewhere an' doin' nuthin'? Like he don't really got no friends. Sometimes I feel sorry for him, man. Me an' Jeffers fuckin' get off more in a hour just curb-grindin' than I ever seen him do."

Donny nodded.

Robby walked to the bed and checked the posters—Iron Maiden, Mega-Deth. There were some drawings too, good ones, with the Tiger-Dog in color. "You do some hot shit, man. The Tiger-Dog should be a sticker!"

Donny pushed the burgers around with a fork, dodging grease spatters. "Um, thanks, dude." He looked up. "Um, you could probably stay here tonight if you wanna . . . The bed ain't very big, but I ain't no homo or nuthin'."

Robby sat on the rumpled bed. It smelled like sweaty-kid and burger grease. "Your mom get pissed?"

Donny flipped the meat. "Naw. But she ask you all kinds of stupid stuff, like where you live an' that sorta shit." He shrugged. "She's really pretty cool, but it might make you feel weird. You could make somethin' up."

Back against the wall by the bed was a good old Santa Cruz Slasher, ridden hard, but dusty now. "Um, that your board, man?"

Donny glanced up. "Naw. That was Duncan's. You can check it if you want."

Robby leaned down to snag it, then stopped. There was dried stuff all over, like old crumbly mud. Robby studied it a long time, but didn't touch it. "Um . . . Duncan get a new one or somethin'?"

Donny didn't look up. Robby hardly heard him above the burger sizzle. "Duncan's dead, man."

Donny mashed the meat hard with the fork. "He jumped off that warehouse by the wharf, man, a few months ago. I found his board in the mud between the rocks next day after the cops leave . . . like he tried to take it with him or somethin'! His mom was a bitch an' I wasn't gonna give it to her! None of the dudes wanted it either. Nobody's rode it again . . . figure the bearings all rusted now anyways. My mom don't like it. She won't even touch it, man!" He opened a cupboard and pulled out a pack of buns. "Duncan was my friend, kinda."

Robby took a big hit of beer. "Sorry, man. I just figured it was yours . . . before you got fat or somethin'."

Donny shrugged. "I always been fat."

Robby drank some more beer and turned to the pictures. Donny could draw to the max! There was one, five dudes on boards, sort of half-cartoon and half-serious. All were black except two, and none looked much over fourteen. One white kid was small and skinny but looked badder than hell. The other was like a total maller, blond and friendly. The black dude in the middle had muscles and it was easy to see he knew what is, is, and what ain't, wasn't worth nothing. That had to be Randers. Another was chubby and did look a little like Robby: Whitey. The last was like the cracker dude at the station, only younger.

Donny came over with two plates and four steaming burgers maxed with stuff and a beer under one arm. He sat beside Robby. "Scarf time."

"Or what!" Robby grabbed a burger and took a huge bite. He turned a little and pointed to the mean-looking white kid. "Weasel, right?"

Donny shook his head. "Naw. That's Kevin. Weasel's the other whitey."

"Don't look like no weasel."

Donny sucked beer and burped. "He put a rat in his mom's microwave once."

"Huh? Oh . . . yeah, right. I think I figured Randers—in the middle and, for sure, he could kick-ass. Who's the skinny dude with the teeth?"

"Rix."

"Ricks?"

"Naw. R-I-X, man. Wait. . . . " Donny slid to the floor and pulled a cardboard box from under the bed. It was full of magazines and had the Tiger-Dog on it. He dug out a Thundercats comic, flipped it open, and pointed to a Moleman. "Rix is the leader of the Molemen. Like, at first they hate the Thundercats an' keep tryin' to kill 'em, but then they get to be friends. There was this big monster-thing tryin' to kill the Molemen an' steal all their stuff an' it kept on blamin' the Thundercats, so Rix starts this big war. Then they finally figure out that they shouldn't be fightin' each other when it's this big monster-thing that's their real enemy."

Robby looked at the picture. The Molemen had huge front teeth. "Shit, they sure don't look friendly!"

"Yeah. Maybe that's why the Thundercats was ascared of 'em at first. Really, they was pretty good dudes behind them teeth."

Robby nodded. "You read a lot, man?"

Donny shrugged and stuck the book back. "Nuthin' else to do 'cept watch TV. The Animals all come up here a lot . . . probably 'cause my mom's not home. She don't mind, really, 'cept I figure she thinks they might not be good dudes, man."

"How come you ain't in the picture?"

"Aw, I drew it. Didn't seem right, y'know? 'Sides, I know what I look like."

"Shit, man. Killer dudes like you Animals could be makin' mega-bucks runnin' rock! There's one board-pack doin' that in Fresno. Even the little kids score a hundred a day just bein' watchers! Fuck. You dudes could have all new boards an' stuff!"

Donny shrugged. "Yeah. There's this bigger kid, fifteen or some-thin', keeps comin' 'round tellin' Randers all that shit. He ain't even old enough for a license an' he drivin' a new Corvette, man! Randers think about it a lot, you can tell. Nathaniel don't like that dealer dude, kicked the shit outta him once. Dude say he gonna kill Nathaniel, only

24

Nathaniel just laughs at him. 'Course, right then, the Animals would've killed the dude anyways, no prob."

Donny went to the fridge and snagged two more Buds. He brought them back, along with a box of Ding-Dongs, and sat. He looked at the old board and then out the window. "Duncan was a Animal then. This dealer dude finally talked him into bein' a runner. No prob an' he was makin' mega-money . . . scored everybody new wheels an' Swiss bearin's an' found some store'd sell him cases of Heinie at three times the price . . . 'cause he was only fourteen still." Donny shrugged. "He got sorta like that Ricky on Silver Spoons—all kinds of shit but nobody liked him much. Then he started into doin' rock himself. Max. Stayed wasted all the time an' didn't even ride no more. Spent all his money an' didn't have no friends. . . . Then he goes an' fuckin' jumps off the buildin' one night, man! Shit! I still wanted to be his friend only he wouldn't let me!"

Robby chugged the rest of his Bud, picked up a second. "Jeez, you gonna cry?"

"Naw!"

Robby ate a Ding-Dong and washed it down with beer. "They got this place in Fresno, man. The dudes call it the Rock House. It's for kids. You go there an' they kinda lock you inside, sellin' you rock an' keepin' you wasted till you don't got no more money. Sometimes they give you food from Burger King." He shrugged. "One dude from school even sold his board so's he could keep goin' there a little more. I don't know, man. Maybe Randers is right? Sometimes I figure I don't know enough about shit, but ain't nobody tells you nuthin'! All that dogshit on TV looks like it's for squid-kids, man!"

"Yeah."

"So, how come this Nathaniel ain't in the picture?"

"Nathaniel ain't a Animal. He could be if he wanted, but maybe the other kids at the Center'd be ascared of him then?" Donny pointed to another drawing. "That's Nathaniel."

Robby looked. The dude was white, with really light blond hair like a surfer, down over his shoulders like a metaler. He was thin but not skinny and his face was hard but not mean. Robby studied the picture a long time. It was only a drawing but the dude was old. He looked about nineteen or something. "I thought you said Nathaniel was a boy?"

Donny ate a Ding-Dong and drank some more beer. "Naw. I said, *kinda.*" He thought a while. "Ain't nobody knows what Nathaniel is. Sometimes he's a boy, but he can be a man when he gots to."

"Kinda like one of them homos that dresses like a kid?"

"Nathaniel ain't no homo, dude!"

"Aw, that ain't what I meant anyways."

Donny nodded and looked back at the picture. Then he whispered, "I figure he's some kinda werewolf."

"Naw! There ain't no such thing!" Robby turned back to the drawing. "Maybe in Germany or somethin'?"

Donny shrugged. "Yeah? Well, it's like he never gets no older . . . like he's gonna be what he is forever. He rides this ancient Hosoi Street board an' shreds to the max!" He chugged the last swallow and got up. "Anyways, if he is a werewolf or somethin', he's the coolest one you'll ever see! He *likes* kids, man! An' not the way all them pervs always tellin' you! He fuckin' *cried* about Duncan, man! Like it was his fault or somethin'! He talks real talk too . . . not like old people with all that dogshit stuff don't mean nuthin'. He ain't no pussy neither! Dude gots a prob, he can tell it to Nathaniel an' he *help!*"

Robby nodded and drank some more. "Wish we had a dude like that in Fresno."

Donny smiled. "I don't figure there's anybody else like Nathaniel anywheres! All the Animals would die for him, man! He don't tell us what to do neither. One time, Randers called slavers on him an' he didn't even hassle about it!"

Robby finished the second Bud. He was a little buzzed and his belly was tight and full. It felt good. "Um, can I score another smoke off you, man? I'll pay you back."

"For sure." Donny held out the pack and they both fired from the Bic again.

"So, what's slavers?"

Donny got up and went to the fridge for the last two Buds. "You don't got that in Fresno?"

"I don't know. Maybe we call it somethin' else?"

"Yeah. Um, say you fuck-up on one of your friends? He gets to call slavers on you an' you got to do anything he wants till he calls it off again. Shit. Randers would call it on you right now just for bein' here!"

"Naw. We got nuthin' like that. If you fuck-over one of your friends or do something hurts all the dudes, you just get beat up."

Donny smiled and handed him a Bud. "Yeah? Slavers is better. The other dudes get to make you do stuff, *any* stuff, or they can just save it back till there's somethin' really gross or scary to get done." He shrugged. "You get your ass wiped an' it's over. Maybe it hurts awhile but no prob. Slavers makes you think about the shit that you done longer an' you don't do it again."

"What if you don't wanna do it?"

"*Then* you get your ass wiped! You wouldn't be a Animal no more either!"

"Sounds like some little-kid shit. You ever get it called?"

"Yeah. Once."

"What'd you have to do, lick dog-piss or somethin'?"

"Naw. *That* would be little-kid shit!" Donny slid to the floor again and pulled out the box. He dug under all the skate magazines and comics and held up a black .45 automatic, then tossed it to Robby. "I had to roust it outta this dealer's car! Right in the street in the daytime!" He giggled. "Weasel helped a little. He threw a big handful of dogshit at the dealer-dude's bodyguard who's 'sposed to be watchin' the car. Right in the fuckin' *face,* man! Weasel booked on his board an' I score the gun while the guard was chasin' him! Dude had a Uzi, I think, but was ascared to use it on the street 'cause it was daytime."

Robby checked the big gun. "This's hot, man! It's like an army one! Jeffers gots this old thrasher .38 but I only seen this kind in movies. Eddie Murphy gots one." Robby held it in both hands and aimed at Donny's chest. He made a gun-sound and Donny grinned and fell back on the floor. Robby checked the gun again—heavy, black, and important as hell. "Ain't nobody gonna kick your ass when you got somethin' like this, man! Um, loaded?"

Donny sat up and held out his hand. Robby gave him the gun and Donny pulled the clip and held it up. "Only seven. 'Sposed to have eight an' then you can keep one in the chamber too, but I shot it once at the old Navy yard to see what it'd feel like." He grinned. "Slams your wrist, man, max!" He shoved the clip back in and threw it to Robby again.

"Awesome! How do you cock it?"

Donny sat on the bed. "Like this." He worked the slide. "Take off the safety. . . . " He did. "An' you ready to waste somebody."

Robby held it in both hands, arms out, finger on the trigger, and looked down the sight. "Wanted to waste this dude at school one time. Kept on beatin' me up . . . for *nuthin',* man! Every fuckin' day!"

Donny nodded. "Yeah. I figure everybody gots somebody they wanna kill."

Robby lowered the gun and looked at it a while longer. Then he handed it back. Donny pulled the clip, worked the slide, and the bullet popped out. He pushed it back in the clip. "Randers said I could keep it. He already gots this huge .44 mag. Duncan give it to him when he was makin' all the money an' still tryin' to stay friends. Randers shot it a couple times. He say it kicks like hell."

"I like yours, man," Robby said. "Maybe I can score one too?"

Donny shrugged and put the gun back in the box, covering it with comics. "No prob if you gots the bucks. Kevin wants a Uzi like the dealers got, but he had to use some of his money to buy a new deck." He glanced at the dusty old board again. "Figure pretty soon he gonna try rock-runnin' too."

There was a clock on a box beside the bed and Donny glanced at it. "Nine-thirty, man. My mom'll be home in a little while." He handed Robby the last Ding-Dong. "She works at this bakery thrift-store; that's how come we always got lots of this stuff." He thought a minute. "Maybe I gots somethin' figured tonight. Chug the beer so's we can dump the empties."

Robby grinned and did. He stood up and fell against Donny, who laughed and caught him. "Hey, dude, three wimpy Buds an' you wasted?"

"Jeez, I ain't had nuthin' to eat in two days, man! What'd you expect?"

Donny held his shoulders. "Yeah? You ain't gonna puke or nuthin'?"

28

"Naw."

Donny kept hold of Robby's shoulders. "Um, I was gonna ask if you wanted to take the cans down to the garbage—climbin' them stairs sucks—but you out-of-it!"

"No I ain't! Shit, I could handle another sixer!"

"Yeah, right, dude. Get in bed against the wall. I'm so big mom'll never figure there's two kids in there. She might come over an' kiss me or somethin' but you just keep your head covered. Okay?"

"Or what." Robby pulled off his shirt and Donny had to catch him again.

"You totally ripped, man."

Robby laughed and fell back on the bed. He kicked off his Pumas. "Yeah? I wish I was like this all the time! No probs *for*-ever!"

Donny grinned. "Yeah. Be right back."

"I'm cool."

The window was open a little and that strange/familiar sea-smell drifted in on the breeze and played over Robby's body. He slid off his jeans and it felt good. Once in a while things didn't seem so bad, but it helped to be a little wasted. He was almost asleep when Donny came back and nudged him.

"Get under the blanket, dude."

"Huh? Oh, yeah, right."

Donny turned off the TV and the light, slid off his jeans, and climbed in the bed. Robby snuggled his head on the pillow. Donny's big body gave off heat like a radiator and the kid-smell was good. Except for the burger grease. Donny smelled a lot like Jeffers.

"Um, Robby?"

"Yeah?"

"Um, *you* ain't no homo, are you?"

"No way, man!"

"Sorry."

"It's cool. Um, Donny?"

"Yeah?"

"Why was you down there by the ocean tonight?"

"I don't know. I go there sometimes when there's nuthin' else to do.

I think about Duncan, I guess. Nobody liked him anymore, but he used to be a pretty cool dude."

"Ain't your fault he's dead."

"Yeah. But I still think about him a lot. Nobody gives a shit, man."

"Or what. Um, I'm sorry I called you fat."

"That's cool. Night, man."

"Night."

The Ship

"Hey, you little fuck!"

Kevin didn't even look. He ran—fast—clutching his skateboard by the front truck. No time to deck. Too much garbage anyway.

"Come back here, you little shit!"

Did a coyote *think* about running from a wolf? No way! He booked or got his ass wiped; no shame, no nothing. Fact of life.

"Get back here, fucker. Gonna ream your ass, you little shit!"

Kevin'd seen reamers at the shipyard. He ran, twisting between a rusty dumpster and spilled trash cans. There was a whistle past his ear and a bottle exploded on grimy brick and something stung his cheek like a yellowjacket. His head hurt—it almost always did—and this kind of shit wasn't helping. Howling echoed down the alley, breaking voice, half-man, half-boy, dusted, or something. "Fuckeeeerrrr!"

Kevin ran. He was good at it even if his head did hurt like hell. He didn't know if the dude was following, and wasn't going to look. Ahead, a garbage truck rattled, rusted sides barely clearing the build-

31

ings, a big black dude in sunglasses riding the ass-end and watching with a grin.

"Go for it, boy," he offered.

There wasn't any place to go but into the packer-trough. Kevin scrambled over the lip, into stuff he didn't even want to think about, and the black dude laughed. "Any fuckin' port in a storm, boy."

Kevin didn't know what that meant; it didn't matter anyway, the duster-howling faded—the prey was gone, like on "Wild Kingdom." Kevin jumped out, slipping in garbage, landing hard on his little ass. Starbursts popped bright in his head. The black dude broke up. "Have a nice day, boy." The truck bumped away like a bored dinosaur.

Kevin sat there for a while. Why not? Legs hugged in thin arms, head buried between, and mongrel-blond hair in tangles. His jeans were kneeless and tight over huge dirty Nikes. The Oakland air was already hot and he panted like a dog while his head played blaster music.

"Got a quarter, kid?"

Kevin's eyes peered blue from under long shag and he snagged his board. What the fuck now? Across the alley, an old wino sprawled against the bricks. He didn't look like he'd be booking for a while.

"Fuck you, asshole," Kevin said.

The wino scowled and floundered a little, but Kevin'd been right.

"Eat shit an' die," Kevin added.

The wino bawled ancient curses—Kevin'd heard them all before— old as the fucking hills, and twice as dusty. He got slowly to his feet, huge Nikes a stable base for a little tower of hurt. His mouth tasted like beer puke, and some still crusted his nose. He dug it out, looking toward the street and down the hill where one rusty cargo mast was all he could see of the ship.

His head *really* hurt now.

There was stickiness on his cheek and his fingers came away bloody. He wiped at his face with a handful of the black Iron Maiden T-shirt he wore. His eyes ached when he glanced back, over tarred roofs that shimmered, to the Bay. Then, he dropped his eyes and walked to the alley mouth, hurting too much to ride. Horns honked and exhaust fumes made him want to puke again. Why did he feel so fucking sick all the time? Did other kids feel like this and just weren't saying anything? He turned once, flipping off the wino, but the old douche-bag didn't notice.

A bus was grinding up the hill as he walked down. Smoke blew black, diesel screamed, hurting his ears, and the big stupid thing was helpless. Kevin checked the street but there wasn't a cop escort in sight today. He snagged a bottle from a doorway and threw it as hard as he could. It shattered against a window, starring the glass totally; getting a scream from some fat black lady and a birdo and silent curses from the driver. Kevin decked and rolled. The hill made it easy.

Two blocks down, he could see the ship better out in the dirty water—both cargo masts and the rusty wheelhouse. He gave it a long glance before tailing in a doorway. Then he climbed narrow box stairs that squeaked and smelled like piss, pushing hard on each knee with his hand to keep his legs going, when he really felt like just sitting down and crying. Two floors up the hallway sagged dim in dirty-window light. From the far end came sounds of an old Zoom re-run . . . happy kids singing, "I wanna zooma, zooma, zooma, zoom. . . . "

Yeah, right, Kevin thought, the fuck out of here, for sure.

The door looked like somebody'd tried to kick it in more than once. He knocked, but got nothing but TV giggles.

He pounded, adding a kick. "Donnneee, fucker!"

A chair creaked, chain rattled, and the door dragged back on loose hinges, in a groove it'd scraped in the floor.

Donny was black, and fat to the max. He had a huge hanging belly and big sagging boobs any girl would be stoked with. He only wore jeans, as usual, and they hardly fit anymore, strained across his ass, side seams split, and unbuttoned three from the top so his belly could roll out. He had big white teeth, eager eyes, and a face like a happy pit-bull pup. He carried a slopping bowl of Fruitloops in one hand, and smelled like hamburger grease—the whole room did. He grinned at Kevin. "What's up, dude?"

Kevin pushed past. "Nuthin'."

"Yeah? You look like warmed-over death, man."

"Yeah, right."

There was an old fridge in the kitchen corner. Kevin stumbled over and yanked open the door. Three Buds stood among the other stuff and he grabbed one.

"Hey!" Donny bawled. "My mom kick ass if you drink all them again."

Kevin ripped the tab and sucked, slumped against the door, coughing once and spattering his chest. "Aw, I'll score you some more before she gets home." He killed that one and grabbed another.

"Better," Donny muttered, walking back to the big chair in front of the TV and plopping down. The Zoom kids were talking Ooby-talk.

"Aw, uuuk-fay oo-yay, duuude!" another voice called from the floor.

Kevin turned to see Duncan sipping beer between Donny's sprawled legs and trying to tighten a truck on his thrashed old Slasher skateboard with a pair of pliers. "The world is dogshit," Duncan added.

Donny giggled.

Duncan was fourteen, a year older than the others, shirtless, in faded jeans, tangles of dark brown hair almost as long as Kevin's, and a faint smudge starting on his lip. He was tanned and muscled like a surf-nazi. "Figure you can score them beers quick?" he asked. "I'm bored . . . wanna get totally wasted." He laughed. "Like you are *all* the time, man!"

Kevin picked up his own board and wandered to the window. He could see the ship a lot better from up here. The tide was turning, and it was swinging around slow, but still faced the scrapyard.

"I guess," said Kevin.

"Yeah?" said Duncan. "Don't sound so stoked about it. Figured *you* lived on that stuff."

"Yeah?" said Donny. "Better'n livin' on rock, like you do, man."

"What's *that* supposed to mean, dipshit?" Duncan demanded.

Donny glanced away.

Duncan looked like he wanted to spit, but turned back to the TV. Kevin came over and leaned on Donny's chair, watching too. Some big chubby squid-kid in a captain hat who was really too old to still be with the others, was talking about dolphins or something. There were ships in the background, and an island, with water as blue as a swimming pool.

"Dogshit! Turn to the Thundercats, man!" Duncan said. He reached for the knob.

"Leave it on," Kevin said.

"Yeah? Wanna make me? Or you too fuckin' wasted to fight already?"

"Chill-out, dude," Donny said.

Kevin's eyes narrowed. "Leave it on, dick-breath!"

"Yeah! Leave it!" Donny said.

Duncan looked at Kevin and Donny a minute, then made a throw-up noise, slumped back, and chugged the last of his beer. He shoved Donny's leg. "Move, asshole. Fuck, your feet stink!" He fired a Marlboro.

Donny shifted a little, spooning Fruitloops.

The Zoom kids were back in the studio again, talking Spanish.

Kevin went to the window. "Aw, turn it if you want."

"Yeah, turn it," Donny said.

"Fuck, I'm bored," said Duncan. "Where the fuck's all the other Animals?" He got up and went to the fridge, snagging the last Bud.

Kevin gazed out the window. "Maybe they heard *you* were here, man."

Duncan looked at Kevin's back a minute, then held out the beer. "Um, hav-ses?"

Kevin nodded. Donny looked up. "Hey, c'mon." He struggled to his feet and grabbed at the can in Duncan's hand. "My mom'll have a *cow!*"

Duncan grinned and held the can over Donny's head. Donny looked at Kevin. "You sure you can score some more today, man?"

Kevin sighed. "Yeah."

Duncan tossed the Bud to Kevin, then wrestled Donny to the floor, holding him down. Donny fought and squirmed. Kevin popped the can and tapped Duncan's shoulder with it. "You oughta get laid, dude. Get off Donny before you cream your jeans."

Duncan looked up. "Hey! I been laid lotsa times!"

"Yeah? Tryin' to butt-fuck Donny don't count."

Duncan jumped up and gave Kevin a push. "Hey! I ain't no homo, asshole."

Kevin stepped forward. Duncan was bigger, but he moved back.

"Yeah?" Kevin said. "Then keep your dick away from other dudes."

Duncan looked down. "I don't, man."

"Do," said Donny.

Duncan turned away. "Aw, fuck you both."

Kevin sipped the Bud. Duncan spun around. "You gonna score some more, or what?"

"I said I was. Thought I said it. Felt my lips move when I said it!"

"Yeah? When?"

Kevin shrugged. "Now, I guess. You dudes gonna stay here all day?"

"Or what," said Duncan. "Nuthin' else happening anywheres. Donny's too fat to do anything, an' I never see the other Animals no more. Sit here an' watch little-kid TV." He started to turn away, then stopped and picked up his board, looking at Kevin. "Um, wanna use mine, dude? Just scored new Powell bearings."

"Naw . . . thanks anyway, man."

Duncan shrugged, then glanced at Donny. "All right by me! He'll just get all wasted an' fall off anyways, like he always does." He dropped back to the floor in front of the TV.

Kevin pulled off his shirt and went into the bathroom. Donny followed, watching while he splashed water on his face then soaped under his arms. He offered Kevin his gap-toothed Afro comb.

"Um," said Donny. "He did try homo stuff on me. Two times."

Kevin tugged at his hair with the comb. "Next time, kick him in the balls, dude. You don't got to take that shit. Nobody gots to take that shit!"

Donny nodded, touching Kevin's arm. "Um, I like you, Kev."

Kevin glanced at him and smiled a little. "Yeah? You're all right yourself, home-boy."

"Um, you don't got to score the beer if you don't feel good. My mom just have a old cow, an' she does that all the time anyways."

Kevin sighed. "Got to get it sometime, why not now?"

Donny nodded slowly. "Yeah. Um, what you do to your cheek? It's all bloody."

"Aw, some fuckin' duster threw a bottle at me."

"Jeez. I fix it, man, warp-speed." Donny leaned over and knocked stuff around in the cabinet until he found a tired-looking bottle of Bactine. Kevin tried to dodge, but Donny squirted his cheek with it.

"Fucker!" Kevin hissed.

"Aw, don't even sting."

"Does so, dipshit," Kevin smiled. "Good old Doctor Donny, or what."

Kevin combed his hair. In the other room, Lion-o was telling Panthro about Thundercat honor.

Kevin held his shirt to his nose. "Um, can I use one of yours, dude? Mine stinks. Maybe your Def Leppard one?"

"For sure. That my favorite too. It, um, gonna be kinda big for you."

Kevin checked himself in the mirror. "That might be even better. Make me look smaller. I'll try an' be careful with it."

"Thanks, Kev."

"For what? It's your shirt, lame-o."

"Nuthin'."

Kevin slipped into Donny's big black shirt that smelled like Tide and hamburger grease. He walked back to the window. The tide was coming in and the ship was swinging toward the open sea. The anchor chain was huge.

"Take your fuckin' time, why don't ya," Duncan said.

Donny spun around. "Yeah? Why don't *you* score the fuckin' beer, lame-o!"

Duncan looked at Kevin and smiled a little. "Kev's better at that kinda stuff."

Back on the street, Kevin rolled down toward the docks. First thing, he walked to the end of a rotting wharf and looked at the old ship. The bow pointed out where the other ships were going, maybe to islands with dolphins? In the scrapyard big hammers beat and torches burned laser-blue.

Kevin walked back to the street and sat on the curb in front of a bar. An ancient Steppenwolf song played faintly. He stood his board against a fireplug and pulled up his legs, looking small and alone. The day dragged. It got hotter than hell, and stink blasted from the sidewalk. Several cars had slowed, checking him, maybe, but he figured it was going to be a long day. Sweat trickled from under his hair and made his cheek burn. He wished his head would just stop hurting for even a little while. The fireplug dripped and he washed his cheek. A cop car cruised past once; he got a disgusted glance from behind dark glasses and it rolled on.

Then, there was a blue Beamer—that was hot!—coming to a nervous crawl, almost taking off again, finally stopping. The engine still idled fast like it wasn't sure. There was a dude, not that old, probably a Silicone, with mirror sunglasses like bug's eyes. "Uh, you know the way to 880, kid?"

Kevin looked confused and got up. He ruffled his hair and stretched, so his belly sucked in—jeans slid down narrow hips, shirt climbed his ribs—would've, if he'd been wearing his own, he had to help Donny's. He pointed. "Um, I think it's up that way, mister."

The dude considered, quick, checking the street, twice. "Uh, would you have time to come along and show me, little guy?"

Kevin looked more confused, and shuffled his big Nikes. He rolled his hands up in the front of his shirt.

"Uh, it's okay, little guy—really. I could even pay you something." The dude smiled. "That's a neat skateboard."

Dogshit old thrasher, Kevin thought. "Um, I guess so, mister."

The dude popped the door and Kevin climbed in with his board. They drove. The car had AC, but it'd just been turned off. It started to get hot inside, even with the windows open.

"Sure is a warm day, huh, little guy?"

"Um, yeah, mister."

The dude pulled off his clean white Computerland T-shirt. His body was white, chubby like a little kid's almost, and his hands were soft. Both he and his car smelled like shave-cream or something and there was one of those Garfield air-fresh things dangling from the Blaupunkt knob. The dude smiled. "That's a lot more comfortable now. Uh, why don't you take yours off, too? You'll feel better."

I doubt, Kevin thought. He gave the dude a little-kid smile and did, wadding Donny's shirt between his leg and the door, so he could grab it fast.

"You dig on rock music, little guy?"

Kevin glanced at the tape tray—ancient history—fucking Beatles even. "Um, KRQR's kinda cool, mister." Kevin found it quick on the radio dial. They cruised slowly along the docks. About a mile ahead was the old Navy storage yard, abandoned now. Kevin figured the dude had already checked it out.

"Damn, it's hot, isn't it, little guy? Look how you're sweating. Uh, what's your name anyway?"

"Timmy."

"Mine's Jim."

Yeah, right, Kevin thought.

"Uh, would you like a beer, Timmy? Your folks mind if you drink beer?"

Kevin gave him a sly smile. "Um, I never tell 'em nuthin'. That'd be really cool, Jim. One time my big brother give me a beer. You, um, kinda look like him." Gotcha, duuude!

Jim pulled his Beamer over at the last little market on the street and gave Kevin a pat on the shoulder. "Be right back, Timmy."

For sure, he took the keys, and the glove-box was locked, but the radio played anyway. Kevin yawned and stretched. His head still hurt, but that would soon be covered. In the outside mirror he could just see the masts above the warehouse line.

Jim came back, sweating, but still smelling clean. He had a sixer of Heineken. Kevin drank one fast while it was still ice-cold. The old chink who owned this place wasn't afraid to spend a little buck keeping his boxes cold. Jim watched him from the corner of his eye; Kevin figured he'd better be cool and slow down for the next one. They drove again. Kevin pointed. "Um, I think the freeway's back up there, Jim."

Jim smiled and gave Kevin's shoulder a friendly squeeze. "Oh, I've got plenty of time, Timmy. You really look thirsty. Want to just cruise awhile, listen to tunes, and drink the beer?"

"Um, for sure. You're a cool dude, Jim." Kevin opened another Heinie. His head felt a lot better now. Jim put a big-brother hand on his leg. "You live around here, Timmy? It looks like mostly colored kids live here. Don't you get lonely?"

Kevin thought a minute. "Naw, I'm just visitin'."

Jim patted his leg. "Going to be around long?"

"Um, I don't know."

Jim smiled. "I like kids, Timmy. I always wanted a little brother." He stroked Kevin's chest. "You've really got a set of muscles for a little guy."

Yeah, right. Me and Wilycat! Kevin eased back in the seat and sipped Heinie. Maybe the dude would put the AC on again? This squid should be good for a case and a ride back to Donny's if he wasn't scared driving his Beamer where "colored" kids lived.

It was dusk when the blue Beamer stopped for a second in the street—just long enough for Kevin to slide out with his board and Donny's big shirt wrapped around two twelvers of Bud. "Next Sunday then, Timmy?" Jim called.

Kevin nodded. "If I can." Yeah, what else am I gonna do, mow the fucking lawn?

"Hey! Kev's back, an' he gots it to the max!" Donny yelled to Duncan as he dragged open the door.

"Yeah? Took the fucker long enough! 'Course, usually he can't walk by now."

"Aw, pull my hose, man," Donny said, as Kevin came in.

Duncan mashed another Marlboro out under the chair. "Your mom still get home around ten, man?"

Donny nodded.

"Hot! Let's book somewhere an' get totally wasted."

Kevin put the twelvers on the table. Donny ripped one open and stuck four cans back in the fridge. "Thanks, man."

Kevin smiled a little. "Anytime."

Duncan came over and popped one. "Hey, asshole!" said Donny. "Tell Kev thanks at least!"

Duncan made a face. "Thanks."

Kevin walked to the window and looked out through the night toward the Bay.

"Well? We goin' or what?" Duncan asked Donny.

"Aw, I don't know, man. Kev's pretty wasted already . . . "

"Aw, fuck him. We can always drag him up to kid-Center place an' leave him there tonight, or do you like him better than me now?"

Donny thought a while, then finally nodded. "Yeah. Figure we could do that."

Kevin stared at the Bay. The old ship was only a shadow. It didn't even have an anchor-light. No reason for one, it was shoved out of the way where no other ships went.

Passing Rite

WHO the hell would want two hubcaps off a '63 Rambler?

Chuck stood in the thick Oakland morning fog and stared at his thrasher car. They'd been on last night, home in Pacifica—he remembered seeing one glint in the streetlight—and for sure nobody over there would want them. Now he'd just walked up a couple blocks for coffee and they were gone. Since the car only had two when he'd bought it for seventy dollars (and Leese said he'd paid too much) it now had zero.

Zip, asshole, he told himself. He crumpled the styrofoam coffee cup in his fist, almost tossed it in the car, then glanced around at the trash-strewn sidewalk. He let the cup drop into the gutter with the rest of the garbage.

The fog made his nose run and he wiped it, studying the car, trying to see it like one of these street-kids would: chalky paint, rusted-out panels, and narrow old stock tires worn so thin nobody'd want them. It had a cracked windshield too; he'd be getting a ticket for that soon. He didn't give a damn about the car—a fuck about the car. Or the hubcaps. Maybe, though he was still having trouble with the idea that there was nothing personal about getting your stuff rousted. But, who'd want the goddamn hubcaps? Unless the kids were just fucking with him again. . . .

Stupid question. But then, over here, most of his questions were stupid and he tried not to ask any. Like, what did it mean when you shared a Marlboro with a naked thirteen-year-old boy?

Christ, he hated that car! One of these days it was going to croak right in the middle of the Bay Bridge, and he'd leave it there. He had to park in the street at home because his parents didn't want it leaking oil in the driveway, or maybe they thought it had some kind of Oakland death-virus sticking to it—like his mom always washed his Oakland clothes separately. At least she hadn't started wearing gloves yet. The neighbors weren't stoked. The same assholes next door who laughed when he kept falling off the goddamn skateboard. But, fuck 'em and feed 'em fish! Someday the cops would sneak by and tow the car because for sure it didn't belong in that neighborhood, just the same as they'd run any of these kids out fast. The whole thing made a totally stupid movie, considering he had a Beamer in the carport. Even stupider was that he was driving the Rambler more and more over there because it pissed everybody off. Christ, old-man Thomas next door always bragged how he went through seven kinds of hell in Vietnam, and now a rusty Rambler almost gave him vapor-lock.

The Beamer wasn't even new, a cheap little 2002 Chuck'd bought used in his sophomore year at high school. He'd driven it over here once, the first day. Naturally, his parents had warned him, and Corey had warned him, BMW meant "break my window" in Oakland. It was a Pacifica joke. But nothing had happened; all day in the stinking street, with beer trucks grinding past, winos stumbling, kids on skateboards, and only about three white faces seen all day, and not even a scratch. Nathaniel had come by on his board that evening just as Chuck was leaving. Arrogant on his stupid kid-toy, Nathaniel didn't even stop, didn't even look really.

"Don't drive it again," was all he said.

And that was about the friendliest thing Nathaniel had said to him in four months.

The fog swirled in wet breeze from the Bay. Chuck hoped it would burn off today. Sometimes it hung around until all the kids had snotty noses and were coughing and spitting. He almost never saw any of these kids in coats, or even jackets.

Chuck gazed through the fog at two stories of crumbling brick. There was a thing up there on the building's front—a cornice? It was cracked as hell, even leaning a little, and one of these days was going to fall right on the goddamn sidewalk, earthquake or not. Kids all over the place and a ton of bricks was going to fall and nobody gave a shit. The whole goddamn world was falling apart and kids played and fought and sometimes even killed each other in the ruins.

And shared Marlboros in bed. . . .

What did that mean?

Chuck looked down. Maybe nothing, asshole, he thought, except to you. Wasn't there an old Bob Dylan song about trying to hide what you didn't know to begin with?

Chuck wanted to believe that. It wasn't any of his goddamn business anyway, but everything these kids did, said, or wore meant something, and it usually wasn't the obvious.

One skateboard gang, the Animals, wore heavy dog-chokers. Another, the Rats, had big chains *welded* around their left ankles. Some of the younger boys wore rags tied on their left knees. Everything was always left. Maybe it was like that ancient fag thing with the earring. Chuck was twenty and it wouldn't seem right to be asking some eight-year-old to explain. Leese knew, Nathaniel knew, but Chuck figured he'd rather ask a little kid than either of them. The stupid thing was they probably figured he just knew anyway.

Chuck leaned against the car and picked paint from a fender. Everything meant something to these kids, no matter how small. No matter what color, they were a new and primitive race evolving fast from garbage, like those scary radical animal sculptures that artist did, the ones that were supposed to inherit the earth someday. Nathaniel never said anything unless it meant something, like, "Don't drive it again." Chuck hadn't, even though Nathaniel was nothing but a big stupid dirty boy who'd probably be dead in five years anyhow, or a lot sooner if one fifteen-year-old snotnose dealer-kid had his way.

Chuck was the only staffer at the center who drove. Leese and the others rode the bus when it had the guts to come down the street and wasn't re-routed because little kids threw stuff or bigger ones shot at it. Then they walked. The kids walked, through dogshit and dealers and perverts and winos and trash. Nathaniel, the Animals, and the Rats rode their boards through the same stuff. Chuck drove a '63 Rambler, Pacifica to Oakland, sometimes seven days a week, where he got minimum wage for three, and meals of government-surplus food—the same crap the kids got—when he had a Beamer in the carport and enough money to eat at McDonald's any time. Worse, he was going to miss the first semester at Berkeley with Corey. Worse still, he was starting to wonder if he was doing it for these kids, himself, or Nathaniel. And Nathaniel probably didn't even *like* him.

Stupid movie! Just like Nathaniel and Randers sharing a Marlboro in bed.

Randers? Probably Randy or Randolph; he could check the file but it didn't matter. Randers was Randers until death, which probably wouldn't be long in coming. Real street names weren't cute like in the books and movies. And they made no sense if you didn't have a codebook. The fattest kid around was called Donny, not Albert, and his name *was* Donny. One Animal was called Whitey, and he was black! Trouble was, Chuck knew it all made total sense to everybody here but him.

He picked at the paint some more. Let it rust; match the rest of the goddamn car. Come to think of it, what the hell kind of name was Nathaniel? Chuck pictured some farm back in Mississippi or somewhere a hundred years ago, and a tall, gangling blond kid wearing nothing but overalls. He should've been holding a goddamn pitchfork and feeding chickens. Instead, Chuck's mind put him in cold blue moonlight on a lonely hilltop like some Transylvanian werewolf. Maybe he'd had hippie parents, the kind who named their kids Star or Zack. Chuck ripped a long scab of paint off the fender.

There were heavy steps on wet sidewalk as Leese came up from the bus stop. Chuck hadn't noticed her coming but knew she'd seen him a block away. She looked like a badass Nell Carter who saw everything a block away, just like these kids and Nathaniel. Chuck still had to remember to look, only half the time he didn't know what he was supposed to be looking for. If Leese was pissed about something she'd call him "Chuck." If not, she'd call him "boy." He'd learned that much in four months but still couldn't figure what she meant.

Leese smiled like Nell Carter. "Mornin', boy."

Chuck stopped picking paint and asked the hubcap question.

"Somebody who wanted 'em," Leese said.

Mondays started early. Back in June there were a lot of hungry kids stopping off for free breakfast to get enough energy to fight their way up to War Zone Elementary or Death Camp Junior High. Now, in summer, Chuck figured they just needed the food for simpler reasons like surviving "Street Wars 1990," coming soon to a neighborhood near you!

Three wet ones sat on the steps already. Chuck followed Leese. Corey, Chuck's friend since first grade, wanted to go windsurfing down at Waddell Beach today. Chuck could have, no prob, in a Beamer with a Blaupunkt and Corey—blond, tanned, and muscled like a surf-nazi—beside him. They could score a couple sixers of Heineken from that lovesick old fag at the Quick-Stop, for sure if Corey went in without a shirt. Later, totally buzzed, with a Rush tape on the stereo, they could make it in the car at the beach. Corey's beautiful bod would smell like wetsuit rubber.

One of the kids was little. All were black. The little one looked like he'd already been in a fight and lost; on top of that he had a snotty nose and a bad cough. One of the older boys was so fat he couldn't keep his jeans up or the wet skintight Def Leppard shirt down over his middle. That was Donny, the fifth Beatle, the sixth Animal. Chuck glanced at the other boy who gave him a curious look. Chuck shrugged. He was used to getting curious looks. That kid was Whitey. Maybe one of these days he'd ask about that name. Jeez, the little dude looked at him like he'd never seen him before. Maybe the Animals had rousted those goddamn hubcaps.

More kids would come soon, a lot more. What the hell else was there for them to do around here? Some would be on something, some would smell like beer, some would just be lonely, most would be bored, and *all* would have that feeling that something, somewhere, was totally wrong.

He'd learned that much in four months too. When you gave a shit about something, you had to deal with it. People had lots of ways of dealing with things that were discomforting. A Pacifica joke: why did they build the Oakland Bay Bridge? So niggers could swim to San Francisco in the shade.

Chuck followed Leese down the hall. She flipped a switch and old florescents flickered and buzzed. Donny waddled to the main room, Whitey following and looking around like he found new interest in the place. The other Animals would probably come later. They were on Dawn Patrol, though Chuck knew they didn't think like that. Skateboards skidded on wet sidewalks but they'd ride anyway, wet and proud, with scraped knees and elbows they never cleaned or bandaged—kid-warriors, bloody and snot-nosed, in a kid-world that was falling apart, where the guns and bullets were real. Dungeons and Dragons for keeps.

Chuck and Corey used to play Dungeons a lot. Corey even subscribed to a magazine about it. They'd spent long summer days in Chuck's room, door locked, Rush on the stereo, maybe a doober, with the AC on vent. They hadn't really known what they were back then; just two boys who liked each other.

Donny was an Animal by courtesy or something, though Chuck couldn't figure why. He could no more ride a board than run a half block or fight, and he didn't even seem very bright. Being an Animal was having a Gold Card around here.

The Rats would probably come too. Even though the Center was really in Animal ground there seemed to be some kind of treaty. Gang stuff mystified Chuck. At times it seemed so goddamn formal . . . especially for kids who Chuck's mother would say had all the manners of ferrets in a snake pit. There were only four Rats, and for sure the Animals could've kicked their asses anytime, yet they respected each other's boundary marks and even talked once in a while at the center. Three of the Rats were black. One, Chuck wasn't sure, but wasn't going to ask. Like the Animals, they were all around thirteen.

Another was a strange, slender, wiry boy called Eric. Somehow he managed to look gentle without being wimpy. He did funny little magic tricks and spoke so seldom and so softly that Chuck almost never heard him. Yet nobody ever hassled Eric, and yeah, that meant something too.

Nathaniel might be upstairs. He had a room there.

"Boy! I said I need the file on the Danforth kid. Whitey."

"Uh?" said Chuck. "Oh, yeah, right." Whitey was black. Weasel was the friendliest Animal, Whitey was black, and Nathaniel was an obsolete and totally stupid name.

The building was warm. That used to surprise Chuck because it had radiators squatting in corners and some kind of boiler-demon that hissed in the basement with an old black dude to serve it. In books and movies radiators never worked. They were big ugly cast-iron art-deco creatures with clawed feet. They shed aluminum paint like kid-scabs. Some drooled little steaming drops into coffee cans that Chuck emptied. Some, upstairs, like the one in Nathaniel's room, always had a whiff of sulfur-smelling vapor breath trailing from a brass thing. They made netherworld noises and all worked perfectly and the building was warm with that wet kid and dirt smell of a school.

Other kids were coming in now. The little ones went to the little-kid room to watch the Thundercats. Nobody but Chuck called it the little-kid room and there was nothing stopping the little kids from going to the main room; they just didn't. Until, one day, one would, and stayed. If there was some kind of passing rite, Chuck hadn't seen it.

He glanced in to make sure the old TV had warmed up okay so the kids wouldn't screw with it. In a while, the kitchen lady, A.J., who did look like Aunt Jemima, would cook up some oatmeal which went into plastic bowls, and only the really hungry kids would eat. She'd also heat some government crap called MEATFOOD PRODUCT from big cans. A slimy-looking slice of this went on white bread with mayonnaise, and Chuck would bring it all around along with styrofoam cups of bluish milk made from government powder. A lot of the kids liked coffee. Chuck figured Leese bought that out of her own pocket.

Every kid got one of each. Donny got two; the Animals saw to that, especially Kevin. If Donny didn't get two, another Animal, usually Kevin, would give him his. Without his shirt you could count Kevin's ribs. Donny's mom worked at some bakery thrift-store and Donny always had old Ding-Dongs or Twinkies, yet Kevin or another Animal would give Donny his food.

Chuck didn't ask.

More kids came in. They were almost all boys. Sometimes Chuck wondered where the girls went. They were mostly black, mostly wet, and every other word in their language was "fuck." Two were Rats: Mason, the leader or whatever the word was, just on the edge between looking big and bad or fat and dumb; and a smaller boy in tangled dreads who might've been part white, who was probably a retard, and who Chuck could never understand. They went to the main room to watch the Thundercats on the other TV or sit around on the floor and smoke, look at magazines or comics, and talk in the language Chuck didn't understand much more than the retarded kid's, but where every word and tone meant something.

There was a hell of a lot of difference between "fuck you, man" and "*fuck* you, man!"

The files were upstairs and Chuck stopped at the bottom. Maybe Nathaniel was too. He might've been out on the street drinking beer with the Animals most of the night. That was another stupid movie: Nathaniel must've been twenty-something, even if he looked nineteen, yet he'd sit on some dumpster drinking Budweiser that thirteen-year-olds had scored somehow—not that scoring beer was any major prob for kids even in Pacifica. But, what the hell could you talk about with little kids? And Nathaniel talked to them like equals! Of course a lot of it was skateboard stuff. That was another dialect of *the* language. But what could kids have really important to say?

And Nathaniel was "contributing to delinquency." Chuck smiled. Yeah, right! Bud was a lot better than crack, given a choice, and it was a little late for all that TV "be smart, don't start" crap over here. Anyway, Nathaniel seemed to have sort of primitive Dungeon and Dragon code that kept most of the kids out of too much trouble.

But it was still a stupid movie.

A claw-footed radiator lurking in the shadow of the staircase made a demon sound and Chuck emptied its coffee can in the bathroom, then climbed the stairs. From the main room came the voice of Panthro. The kids over here liked Panthro better than Lion-O. In Pacifica it was the other way around.

Chuck looked small but wasn't. He was thin except for a little roll of chub at his belly that Corey ragged him about. He was drinking too goddamn much beer lately. He'd even bought a pack of Marlboros last week, when he'd managed to get all the way through school without smoking. He was white, with long black hair and blue eyes and wore old Nikes, ragged jeans that were clean, and a plain white T-shirt under a Levi jacket that matched the jeans exactly. He had a heavy chrome chain around his neck that looked like a dog-choker but the kids knew wasn't. Corey had given it to him for graduation. He'd bought Corey a case of Heineken and they'd both gotten totally wasted and cruised Highway One clear down to Carmel that night, listening to a Journey tape in the Beamer he hardly drove anymore.

Chuck had muscles but looked more like a happy seventeen-year-old girl in boy's clothes than anything else. He liked who he was and how he looked and there was Corey and what seemed like an infinite California summer ahead . . . until about four months ago.

Over here, most of the little kids liked him; most of the older ones didn't, and the Animals and Rats left him alone because Nathaniel probably said to. Chuck still heard a lot of dusty fag jokes told by kids—"found face-down in the Hudson. . . . " Like nigger jokes, nobody ever seemed to think up new ones.

Chuck pulled the Whitey-kid folder from the file-room cabinet and had to pass Nathaniel's door. It was shut but never locked. It hadn't even been closed all the way last week when Nathaniel was fog-wet and shirtless on his narrow government-surplus bed, huge dirty Cheetahs sprawled on the gray government-surplus blanket, and Randers, black, beautiful, and naked, beside him. Wet clothes steamed and stank on the radiator and Randers shivered against Nathaniel. Nathaniel was reading a Thundercats comic aloud, and that was stupid because he could hardly read, tracing the simple words with a long finger while Randers listened in awe and looked at the pictures and shared a Marlboro.

Chuck read to the little kids and they laughed and giggled. Randers looked like he was listening to the goddamn Bible! Like there was a sacred message in a comic book just because Nathaniel was reading it. Nathaniel hadn't even looked up. Randers gazed right through Chuck and put the cigarette back in Nathaniel's mouth, maybe so he wouldn't lose his goddamn place. A bare bulb burned overhead, and Nathaniel's long body glistened. Randers looked like a Godlet or something. Chuck muttered a "sorry" and closed the door that wasn't, forgetting why he'd opened it in the first place.

Leese looked up under the sputtering florescent as Chuck came in with the folder. As usual, her desk was buried in crap. There was a little plastic sign that read, "They also serve, who do God's will in hell." She looked busy but studied him a moment. "What's eatin', boy?"

Chuck considered stupid questions. "Why's the Danforth kid called Whitey?"

Leese gave him a look like a big Obi Wan who just got asked what Kotex was for. " 'Cause, once upon a time, his name was Whitney. Stupid name for a boy, huh?"

Chuck shrugged. "Oh."

Leese gave him a narrow-eyed glance, but a little boy came running in. "Russel throwin' up! Right on the goddamn floor!"

Leese rose. *"Again?"*

Chuck waved her back, following the boy downstairs where everything was history in the little-kid room except beer-puke on the floor and an eight-year-old with his face in it. Chuck carried him to a chair, then got a wet rag from A.J. and cleaned him up. The boy was totally out-of-it anyway, so Chuck left him there while he got the bucket and mop. Leese was in the hall. "It's over," Chuck said, adding, "*all* over."

Drunk kids were no prob, but there were dusters who raised hell. Dust had been "out" in Pacifica for years except for a few hard-core metalers. Over here, smack was even still in, and crack was killing kids to the max. A big black cop, who looked like he'd seen every movie twice and really didn't want to see one again, brought in a few kids every week who were on something and losing-it. Leese or Nathaniel handled them. Maybe it saved the cop paperwork? Maybe it saved the

51

kids? Nathaniel and the cop talked a lot in the language, but it never looked like they thought much of each other. The cop had never said anything to Chuck, though he couldn't have missed the Rambler's cracked windshield.

Chuck washed the puke off his hands then carried around the food and milk. The kids got their own coffee from A.J. Sometimes Chuck wondered if they got off on having a white dude serve them. He told himself, if his mind had a mouth, it should be washed out with soap.

Donny took his two. Once, Chuck had given Kevin two. But that hadn't worked. Kevin had only sneered—he was good at it—and Donny had gotten three while Kevin ate his like a starved rat then went right back to doing something to his board. Chuck had never figured there was that much to a skateboard; he and Corey hadn't ever been into skating. Here, boards were a lot more than toys and needed constant tuning and maintenance. Chuck hadn't figured they were so hard to ride either. He'd bought his a month ago, a good old street-scarred Alva—he'd learned that much in four months—at the Coliseum flea market from some smart-ass blond Silicon kid who knew goddamn well Chuck didn't ride. Chuck was beginning to wonder if he was too old to learn. That was a new and scary thought.

Whitey took his food and said, "Thanks, man." That was a first! Chuck glanced at the kid. He looked like he'd lost some weight, but he seemed more cheerful than ever before. Chuck shrugged and said, "For sure."

The main room was filling with wet kids now and the language echoed off the high ceiling where old fluorescents flickered dim in cigarette smoke. Only tobacco was allowed. A kid might give Nathaniel a little shit, but nobody messed with Leese. The walls had rock and skate posters, and Leese had let the kids spray paint pictures. Both the Animals and Rats had done their gang-marks . . . equal size and the exact same distance off the floor. The designs were pretty hot considering the medium. Really, dirty wet kids and meatfood product didn't smell bad at all. The first month, Chuck thought the place looked like something out of that Dante book, a break room for off-duty demons. Maybe it was, sort of, but now he found he liked to be there and the kids at least seemed to tolerate him.

He glanced back at Whitey and Donny, who were talking and laughing. Yeah, the Whitey kid had definitely lost weight. Slimer, the retarded Rat, Mason, and number-three Rat, Victor, sat on the floor, smoking and cleaning their boards. Donny and Whitey seemed to be the only Animals around this morning. There'd been another Animal when Chuck had started, a beautiful white boy named Duncan who the cops wouldn't have looked at twice in Pacifica, and who's name should have been Weasel! He was a little older than the others, hard-muscled and bigger except for Randers, and it somehow just didn't look like he fit anymore. One day he never came in and that was the last Chuck had seen of him. Even his name was never mentioned in all that kid-talk. Chuck had almost asked Weasel once, until he thought it over. Leese knew, Nathaniel knew. . . .

Chuck looked in the little-kid room. Russel was asleep in the chair and the others wouldn't hassle him. These kids were cool. He started picking up cups and bowls and plastic spoons.

Nathaniel still hadn't shown.

Chuck stopped a little-kid fight in the bathroom. Nathaniel or Leese handled the big-kid fights, after Slimer kicked Chuck in the balls the first week. Chuck remembered an article in the paper awhile back, about some daycare worker down in Santa Cruz being fired for speaking "in a frightening manner" to a child. Nathaniel's roar could've made a charging panther change its mind, yet five minutes later the kids would be crawling all over him again. Chuck emptied the trash in the dumpster out back. The fog was still thick and wind blew chill from the Bay. The alley stank like rotting cardboard and dead things. Chuck slammed the rusty door. Inside, it was warm and the kid-smell was good. A radiator breathed steam and snickered. Chuck emptied its coffee can. It could've been any normal foggy day.

Some little dude ran to him howling with a scraped knee. Chuck picked him up and hugged him, carrying the boy to the bathroom, snagging the peroxide bottle on the way. Chuck knew he'd have to wash his hair again tonight . . . Leese had told him that dog shampoo killed lice just as well as the special kind and cost about half. She was right. "It gonna hurt?" the boy demanded, as Chuck opened the bottle.

"Maybe a little, dude, but you don't want infection, huh?"

"What's affection?"

Chuck cleaned the boy's knee, pointing out how peroxide foamed on blood. That usually worked. The boy ran back to the TV room, and Chuck stood awhile in the empty hall listening to the kids. "What's affection?" How high is up? Finally, he climbed the stairs and stopped at Nathaniel's door.

He remembered the first day—the first minute. Leese had looked up from his government-printed universal one-size-fits-all application form, which he'd found out later didn't mean dogshit to anybody, except maybe some computer across town.

"Why over here?" she asked. He knew she knew the answer.

Chuck shrugged. "I didn't qualify anywhere else."

Leese nodded. "You like little kids?"

Chuck glanced up. He knew she could've said "boys." And she knew he knew she knew. This big old lady was cool! "Sure . . . I mean, I'm here."

"Mmmm. Why at all?"

Chuck had thought about that one a lot but still wasn't sure. He remembered a few months back. He and Corey were on the bed in Chuck's room, door locked, drinking enough Heinie to keep a buzz. It was hot, even with the AC purring in the window, and they lay side by side, shirtless, shoulders touching, a little sweaty, same as they'd done for years. It just felt good, even when they'd been too little to know why. Two of a kind that the world didn't really want. The TV was on—some special about Oakland street kids and their "plight."

What a wimpy word.

Sunlight shone gold through the window. There were smells of summer lawns. A mower droned somewhere, a sleepy kind of sound. Corey yawned. "Feels like Ferris Bueller's day off, don't it?"

"Or what." Chuck sipped beer and watched the TV. A little black kid, dim against dirty brick, graffiti at his back—a totally staged shot for sure—looked wary on the screen. Some Silicon newslady—she was black too, only the kid acted like he didn't think so—was asking him stupid stuff. Most of the questions should've made her ashamed of herself. There was a close-up of the little dude's face, he couldn't have been more than seven or eight, but Chuck caught a certain glint in his eyes. Chuck sat up and laughed. The little dude was giving that dumb bitch a total ration of shit and she didn't even know it.

Corey wasn't dense. He watched a minute too. "That's one sly little pickanniny there, y'know. Nothing could be that bad in Oakland."

Chuck watched until the scene was over. "I don't think he meant it that way, man. I got the feeling it's a hell of a lot worse and the kid's disgusted with Miss Eskimo Pie for not knowing it."

"Eskimo Pie?"

"Calvin in third-period told me that a few months ago. Black on the outside, white on the inside. Indians say 'apples.' "

"Oh. Well, maybe the little dude's pissed 'cause nobody gives a shit!"

"Yeah," Chuck said. "Standing outside Baskin-Robbins with no money watching everybody else eat could do that to you."

"Nobody gives much of a shit about these kids," Leese said, tossing the application aside. "The media's startin' to call 'em 'damaged,' or 'wilding's' or some other catchy buzzword. Used to be 'disadvantaged' . . . 'bout as appropriate as calling cyanide a 'stomach irritant,' huh?" She leaned back in her chair and it popped. "You'd be working with them alone a lot." It was hot, and street sound drifted in the open window along with tar and exhaust and sidewalk stink. Few of the boys wore shirts and the building smelled like sweaty kids. Leese gave Chuck that up-the-block glance. "Gays, I don't mind . . . " She smiled a little. "Anymore. 'Less they whine about discrimination an' expect me to feel sorry for 'em. Guess I just can't work up much sympathy for anybody feels they bein' discriminated against when all they gotta do is change their clothes or hairstyles to make it stop." She smiled again. "Even those punkers are nuthin' but anti-matter hippies. You want to walk around with a sign sayin' 'kick me,' you shouldn't scream if some people do."

"Well," said Chuck. "It's supposed to be a free country."

Leese yawned. "So they tell me."

Chuck felt his face flushing. "And I hate that fucking word, 'gay!' "

Leese cocked her head. "Oh?"

"Yeah! It makes me think of Christmas! Or some arthritic old homo prancing around like some kind of parody of being a boy. Like, who the hell ever polled *me* and asked what I want to be called, huh?" Chuck spread his hands. "Hey, I did boy stuff, y'know ... fights, bloody noses? I never took homemaking. I wrecked my goddamn bike when I was ten and broke my goddamn arm. Me and my friends walked this big pipe over a canyon, same as the other dudes." Chuck thumped his chest. "Maybe I just blew this job, but I never feel *gay,* lady! For sure I don't have to dress this way. Maybe I should put on an old Oakland Raiders sweatshirt or something? There's this old song by the Who; it goes, 'I'm a boy, I'm a boy!' "

Leese smiled. "I've heard it. I was waiting for you to tell me the one about, if you can't trust a homo around little boys, how can you trust a hetero around little girls?"

Chuck smiled too. "I never heard that one before." He grinned. "Jesus, you figure all us people *know* each other or something?"

"Okay, boy. Spare me how many times you seen Richard Pryor movies." She fired a Lucky and blew smoke. "Most of these kids won't like you an' they got their reasons. Most of 'em are hard, some of 'em are dirty, an' a few got guns an' know how to use 'em. But this's the world we gave 'em an' nobody seems to want to change it. General attitude nowadays is 'I got mine so you get yours' ... an' it come in all colors. Maybe it's hard to believe sometimes, but those rowdy little beasts downstairs are only kids, an' inside they dream the same dreams any kid does. All they'd really like is for somebody to care about 'em a little an', as wimpy as it sounds, to be loved."

Leese smiled again. "You'll probably catch hell for awhile. Forget any child psychology classes you might've took. We had a college girl here a few months back, black too; you'd think she'd of known better. The kids had her in tears the first day. Last I seen of her, little Russel was starin' up in her face with his hands on his hips, squeakin' out somethin' like, 'What I think? I think you go an' FUCK yo'self, bitch!'" Leese studied Chuck a moment. "Russel be eight this month."

Chuck nodded. "I think I see what you mean."

"Well, these kids won't bite, maybe, but they'll test you every way else they can."

"Why?"

Leese blew smoke at the window. "Same reason any kid does—to see if you really give a shit. Don't be afraid to get pissed off and yell like you done a minute ago." She studied Chuck again. "An' don't be afraid to touch 'em. Sometimes I think that's what they need most. You ever see Nathaniel down on the floor like a panther with cubs on Wild Kingdom you'll know what I mean." She waved at the waste-basket. "Right now, you can start dumpin' the trash. Dumpster's in the alley out back. That's A.J. in the kitchen; she won't bite either. An' if you can understand half her rasta talk, it's better than I can do. You'll probably meet Nathaniel prowlin' the halls. I'll show you around when I get time."

Chuck smiled. "Does he bite?"

Leese looked thoughtful. "Maybe when the moon's full."

Chuck grinned and reached for the wastebasket. "Yeah, right."

"You type?" asked Leese.

"No."

She smiled again. " 'Course not. Don't know what I'm thinkin'. What normal boy could type."

That day, Chuck had seen Nathaniel once in the upstairs hall. He was shirtless and carried a thrashed old skateboard. He was tall and thin, with huge feet and hands, like something that'd never quite grown up. There was just enough padding in his frame to keep him from being wiry. He was as hairless as a sixth-grader, streaked with dirt and sweat, and his hair was a long pale metaler mop, almost hiding indigo eyes. For a moment Chuck thought he was just another kid. He looked like a retard, smelled, and somehow Chuck pictured him chained to something by that massive dog-choker around his neck.

Chuck stood at Nathaniel's door. Yeah, maybe back in the old days, on some isolated farm, they might've chained some big retard named Nathaniel in the barn because he howled or something . . . fed him with a big bowl, maybe. He wondered a moment what they did with retarded slave children, damaged wild ones. Shot them? There was a song by Lou Reed, "Boulevard." One of the lines went, "let's just club 'em to death and get it over with." People didn't even do that to otters any more.

Chuck knocked—nothing—and went in.

57

The room was small, probably storage once. The single window was dim and dirty, but the view was only the next building's brick. There was the bed, no sheets, the radiator with its sulfur-steam breath, and an ancient wooden three-drawer file cabinet minus drawers. The top section had two pairs of ragged jeans, heavy socks, and a couple of black T-shirts. The next section had a bunch of skateboard stuff: worn wheels, trucks, bearings, and blocks. There was a little stack of skateboard stickers too. The kids would come up and look through them; they were goddamn particular what went under their decks. The bottom section held some skate magazines, comics, and two cans of Bud. On top of the cabinet was a butt-filled ashtray and a few metal and rap tapes. On the floor was a thrashed old blaster. The walls had rock and skate posters and skateboard stickers. Two stickers on the window read, "When your board is your only weapon, USE IT!" and "Don't Die Wondering." The room smelled like Marlboros and sweat.

Was this where twenty years of "doing the right thing" got you?

Chuck glanced at the stickers again. His parents donated to Greenpeace and had "Save the Whales" and other things like that on the back bumper of their Honda. His mother had given him a small sticker about otters and just to make her happy Chuck had stuck it on the Rambler. One evening, as Chuck was leaving the Center, Nathaniel had spoken another whole sentence to him.

"Y'know?" he'd said, with a strange little smile. "I'd strangle all the fuckin' otters in the Pacific Ocean if it'd bring Duncan back."

Chuck didn't ask where Duncan was, but he'd scraped the sticker off that night.

Chuck sat on the bed and gazed out at the fog. The punkers said "no future," and for sure there wasn't much here. Chuck remembered some books he'd read in school, something about it being the quality of life that was important, not the quantity. But he couldn't see where Nathaniel or these kids could look forward to much of either. They were like lonely wolves in a world where the sheep locked the wolf in a cage and beat it to death . . . slow. There were black sheep too.

He'd read somewhere that wolves were hard to tame and never made good pets.

There was a shadow in the flickering hall light and Eric walked in the open door. He wore no shirt, only a ratty oversize leather bomber jacket with a broken zipper, tattered kneeless jeans, huge old Cons, and the heavy Rat chain around his left ankle. His black eyes seemed large in his narrow face beneath a bushy mop of hair. He was almost more pretty than handsome, yet there was nothing girlish about him. He didn't look at all surprised to find Chuck sitting on Nathaniel's bed.

Eric gave Chuck a smile, then knelt and snagged one of the Buds, glancing up. "Want one, man?"

Chuck smiled too. "Naw. Thanks, dude."

Eric popped his beer, sipped, and looked at Chuck a minute. You couldn't read those black eyes at all. "Why you be sad, man?" asked Eric.

Chuck shrugged. "I don't know."

Eric smiled again, somehow looking like an elf. Chuck wondered why nobody ever imagined that there might be black elves too. "It 'cause you a homo, huh?"

"Probably."

Eric took another sip of beer. "So? Everybody know that. Guess some dudes jus' like other dudes, huh?"

Chuck looked up. Put-ons were something he'd learned a lot about in four months too. But Eric only shrugged. "Nuthin' be wrong with that, I guess, long's you don't go all weirdorama over it. Hey, man, some of the dudes here figure you might be kinda cool anyways, 'cept maybe you don't talk enough."

Chuck studied Eric. Black faces were hard to read, but the kid seemed totally serious. "Yeah? Well, what should I say?"

Eric put a long finger to his forehead. "What be in here."

For a moment, Chuck forgot he was talking to a little kid. "Um, what if it comes out kinda stupid? Y'know, uncool?"

Eric's eyebrows arched. "Cool not half as 'portant like true, man. Anyhow, be stupid, everybody tell you, don't gotta worry over that! But, hey, you not be sayin' nuthin' all the time, how anybody 'sposed to know what you feelin' about 'em inside?" He hesitated a second. "White faces hard to read. Most not look happy."

Chuck grinned. "Maybe just the ones *you* get to see."

Eric laughed. "Hey, that be like what I mean, man! An' be a cool thing too! Anybody read a smile, any color, no prob. An', say stuff like that more." He cocked his head. "You got a 'puter home?"

"Huh?"

Eric frowned a little and tapped an invisible keyboard. "Y'know? A 'puter, man?"

"Oh. Yeah. Only I don't use it much. Just have a few games. Why, you got one?"

Eric laughed again and Chuck thought of black elves. Of course there were! "Get real, duude! School always be talkin' about gettin' some . . . *talkin'.*"

Chuck thought a moment. "Mmmm. Well, mine's just an old Apple. Maybe I'll bring it over, set it up in the storage room or something. I think I still have the training program and manuals."

Eric's eyes sparkled like black ice for a second then turned practical. "Probably get thrashed, maybe even rousted."

Chuck shrugged. "Don't die wondering."

Eric grinned. "Awesome! Um, I gotta book now, but later, dude." He walked out.

Chuck sat there a few minutes longer, then got up and left, closing the door behind him. At the bottom of the stairs he saw Nathaniel coming up the hall with a tall fourteen-year-old boy called Ghost. Both he and Nathaniel were fog-wet and dripping. Nathaniel carried his and Ghost's boards in one hand and half dragged the boy with the other. Ghost was on something and crying like a scared baby. Nathaniel hauled him up the stairs. Chuck gazed after them. He felt like just going into the main room, sitting down on the floor, and letting the warmth and the smoke and the language flow around him.

A little boy, about six, came up with an old book. "Hey! Read me this, man!"

Chuck sighed and smiled. "For sure. Let's go to the kitchen where it's quieter, huh?"

"Yeah!" said the kid, grabbing Chuck's hand. "C'mon!"

Chuck followed him up the hall. "Um, want to hear a joke?"

The kid stopped. "Yeah!"

"Well, there was this boy named Johnny Fuckerfaster. . . . "

The little kid made a face. "Fuck, man! That's *so* old!"

Chuck grinned, almost asking, how old is it, Johnny? "Yeah. Sorry."

The book was a totally thrashed copy of *Where the Wild Things Are*. A.J. liked to listen too, even if she pretended she didn't. Sometimes, she gave Chuck an extra sandwich. That was stupid as hell, but he ate it anyway. The little boy laughed and checked the pictures through the whole thing.

"You know, *this* is old, man," said Chuck.

"Yeah," said the kid. "But it funny! Read it again!"

"Can't. Time for lunch, dude. Dogmeat and tiger-puke."

The kid giggled. "You got it, Toyota."

Lunch included CHEESEFOOD PRODUCT. Chuck carried the stuff around, noticing that Russel and his board were gone. After lunch, Chuck gathered up all the garbage in a trash bag and went back to the alley door. The rusty iron was warm to his touch and glaring sunlight blasted into his eyes as he shoved the door open. Time warped fast when you were having fun. Instead of cold wet dead things, the alley now smelled like week-dead cats being microwaved, and the dumpster lid almost fried his hand when he lifted it. Something like a shiny Frisbee flashed past his head and clattered against the brick wall. He spun around to the sound of kid-laughter—the nasty kind.

A boy sat on a garbage can, casually flipping the other Rambler hubcap, cigarette in his mouth, Heineken bottle in the other hand. He wore clean new jeans, new Airwalks, no shirt, and a gold chain so outrageously huge it had to be real. He looked like a badass Webster who should've gone on a diet last year, and his chubby face wasn't made for the smirk it had. He chugged the last of the beer, burped, smashed the bottle, and slid off, sailing the hubcap at Chuck, who ducked. "Squeaker say he give you twenty bucks for a BJ, man," the kid snickered, then walked away, not looking back.

Chuck watched him—*the* walk. A boy like that should be spanked . . . or shot. Chuck sighed. Well, at least that was one less stupid question. He picked up the hubcaps and went back inside. The radiator was cold now and he leaned on it, considering other stupid questions. Then he climbed the stairs and knocked on Nathaniel's door.

"It's open."

Deja vu, thought Chuck. Nathaniel sat on the bed, wearing only jeans. With his big feet, he looked like Gollum. The room was warm and the window open, but Ghost lay under the single gray blanket, shivering while his clothes were spread on the radiator. He had a cigarette in his fingers but seemed to have forgotten it, and he stared around with wide eyes that found peace nowhere but Nathaniel. One thin hand clutched Nathaniel's arm.

Chuck remembered Eric. "Um, got a smoke, man?" Maybe that wasn't so lame?

Nathaniel had a *Thrasher* open on one knee and a Marlboro in his mouth, half-gone. He pulled out the cigarette, offering it to Chuck and smiling a little. His eyes, usually as unreadable as Eric's, were friendly. "What's up, Alpo?"

"Um. . . . Alpo?"

Nathaniel grinned like a cheerful werewolf. "Nobody told you your name yet? Kinda short for Meatfood Product . . . an' cooler than Dogmeat. Shows they thought about it a long time."

"Alpo?"

Nathaniel raised an eyebrow. "You could do worse. You don't get a name 'less you're worth one."

"I mean, is it good?"

Nathaniel shrugged. "Stuff keeps you alive, don't it? Helps you survive."

Chuck nodded slowly. "Yeah. I guess it does. Um, you need any help?"

Nathaniel smiled. "Lots."

"Um. . . . " Chuck looked at Ghost and made a helpless gesture.

Nathaniel sighed. "He's just dusted a little." He turned and smiled at Ghost. "Ain't ya, dude?" He took Ghost's hand. "Squeaker sell some badass shit, huh?" Nathaniel glanced back at Chuck. "Aw, he can hear us, man. Just, by the time he decides what he wants to say it's gone, y'know? You ever do dust?"

Chuck handed back the cigarette. "No. What's it like?"

For an instant, Ghost's eyes saw Chuck. "Scary," he muttered.

Nathaniel nodded and smiled. "He's baaa-aaak. Leastways, gettin' there." He took a hit off the Marlboro and offered it to Chuck again. "Well, you ever want to try, don't buy from Squeaker. He got his own secret formula. I can almost always tell when some kid's on his shit."

"Don't," said Ghost.

"For sure," said Chuck, taking a hit and handing the cigarette back. "Guess you won't do it again, huh?"

Ghost looked blank. Nathaniel squeezed his hand and smiled at Chuck. "Just give 'em one or two words at a time for awhile. That's all they can handle. Sentences come later in the program." He sighed. "Maybe he won't, maybe he will." He blew smoke and passed the Marlboro.

"Squeaker just sent my hubcaps back," said Chuck. "His bodyguard delivered 'em. Airmail, sorta."

Nathaniel grinned. "Yeah? Aw, that's just the little shithead's way of gettin' attention 'cause nobody likes him no more."

Chuck's mouth opened. "But he's a crack dealer. I heard kids have even died because of him. You make him sound like just another kid or something."

Nathaniel shrugged. "He is. Hell, if you could magic him away someplace where he could get to be a kid for real he'd probably end up just a average fifteen-year-old." Nathaniel sighed. "Only, in this world that never happens. Sometimes I wish I had a huge island. . . . " His voice trailed off.

"You mean you feel *sorry* for Squeaker?"

"No." Nathaniel looked up, his eyes level and unreadable again. "The dude made his choice. He knew what he was doin', an' this ain't Sesame Street."

Chuck thought awhile then nodded, glancing finally at the Marlboro. "Um, this mean something? When you share a cigarette?"

Nathaniel's eyes crinkled a little at the corners and he smiled. Then he turned to Ghost, speaking softly. "Dude wants to know something', man."

Ghost's eyes stopped searching the ceiling and he thought hard. "Alpo?"

Nathaniel gazed into the kid's eyes and nodded. "Yeah. Listen. Alpo wants to know what it means when you share a Marlboro. You tell him?"

Ghost looked confused. "A . . . a Marbro? Share?"

"Uh huh. Just a plain old Marlboro."

Ghost gripped Nathaniel's arm tight. It looked like he was thinking as hard as he could. Once, he looked at Chuck like he figured *he* was on something. Nathaniel gave Chuck another smile. "He thinks it's a trick question. You really shouldn't ask a dude trying to find his way home stuff like that."

Chuck looked concerned. "Um, it's not important, man . . . "

Ghost pointed a finger, struggling to make the words come. "Mean, mean, it mean it the last one in the pack, dipshit!"

Perv

"THAT'S the perv, man!"

Kevin pointed a dirty finger. Three stories down, a big blue Beamer cruised the empty street, slow. The other kids crowded the window, broken glass crunching under ragged Nikes, Cons, and Cheetahs. The Oakland afternoon was late and hot, smelling of tar, garbage, and steamy salt from the Bay. The kids were shirtless, six of them, as they shoved each other, sweaty, at the window.

Randers, almost fourteen and the oldest, pushed between Donny and Whitey. He dropped a hand on Kevin's thin shoulder and spat down at the street. The luche missed the Beamer's roof by inches. "For sure, dude?"

Kevin nodded, eyes locked on the car. "Or what!" His mongrel-blond hair was a dirty tangled mop over his shoulders and back, almost hiding blue eyes that burned fierce now. He spat too, but the car was out of range. "That's the cocksuckin' perv, beat me up, man!"

Behind, Rix leaned over both sets of shoulders, easily because he was the tallest Animal. He was ebony black, more wiry than skinny, with big buck teeth that his lips never totally covered. "Wipe the fucker's ass," he said.

Weasel grinned and nodded. He was the kind of beautiful white boy, tanned, with pale blond hair, that every surf-kid wished he could be. Cops at the mall never looked twice at Weasel. He had strange amber eyes like a coyote and an open friendly face. He had a ragged black T-shirt tied around his waist that said "Smart-ass White Boy" on the front; the Animals had given it to him last year for a birthday present. It was too small now and worn to death. He was jammed between Donny's sweaty bulk and jagged glass in the window frame, but ignored both.

The kids watched as the Beamer cruised the block and finally turned the corner.

"Figure he be back?" Rix asked.

Kevin nodded, still staring at the empty street. "Believe it, dude! He wants a black kid now."

The Animals moved from the window and sat in a circle on the sagging concrete floor around the dead ashes of a little fire. Two quart bottles of warm Budweiser stood nearby. Rix snagged them, popped the caps, and started them around. Weasel dug a pack of Marlboros and a Bic lighter from his pocket. Donny had a squashed box of Ding-Dongs and scooted it toward the middle.

Randers fired a cigarette and blew smoke. His face was a lot harder than the other kids' and even when he was talking he looked like he was already thinking of something else. "Figure I do it," he said.

Kevin smiled a little and shook his head. "Naw, man. Figure. All them muscles, you'd scare the perv away. Jeez, sometimes you look sixteen or somethin'."

"I'll do it," said Donny.

The kids broke up except for Kevin, who only smiled and gave Donny's big shoulder a soft punch. "Thanks, man, but that perv wants a *little* kid."

Donny grinned shyly and looked at the floor.

Rix stood up, but Randers shook his head. "You way too tall, dude."

Weasel took a huge hit from a bottle, a bite of melted Ding-Dong, and looked across at Kevin. "Sure the kid's gotta be black? Hey, that's ... um ... dec ... desc ... "

"Discrimination, dipshit," said Donny.

"Whatever."

Kevin shrugged. "That's what the perv kept askin'; did I know any 'black boys'."

Everybody turned to Whitey, who was the color of Heineken Dark.

"Figure he too fat?" Randers asked.

Whitey patted his belly, which hung a little over his ragged jeans. He had heavy boy-breasts backed my muscle. "Ain't fat," he said. "Mom tell me there just be more to love."

"Yeah?" said Rix. "Then Donny's mom must be totally stoked."

Kevin studied Whitey, then turned to Randers. "I guess we could try it."

The bottle came to Whitey but Kevin snagged it before he could drink. "Perv wants to get you wasted in the car—so's you'll play. Can't already have beer on your breath, man."

"Jeez, I'm thirsty, dammit," Whitey began. Randers gave him a look. Whitey shrugged, glancing at Kevin. "Aw, figure he really gonna cruise back today?"

Kevin spat on the floor, raising a puff of dust. "Look. It's Sunday an' I was too pissed off to be there last week. Figure he's missin' his meat, man. For sure he ain't got balls to be cruisin' for kids in his own Silicone-land." Kevin looked toward the window. "Yeah. He'll be back. Believe it."

Weasel grinned. "Sorta like doin' crackers, huh? You always want a little more?"

Randers frowned. "We got enough probs without be gettin' into that shit!"

"Aw, I didn't mean ... " Weasel began.

"Stand up, man," Kevin said to Whitey.

Whitey rose and stood before the others in a broad bar of sunlight. Dust motes danced around him. Kevin got up and patted Whitey's chest. Whitey grinned. "Homo."

"Shut up," said Kevin. "Suck in your tum."

Whitey did, hardening his chest and flexing his arms.

"Mister Teen-age America or what," Weasel snickered. The others giggled.

"Maybe," said Kevin. "Perv told me once he hated to see all them fat kids around where he lives. Like *he's* Rambo or somethin'."

Whitey let out air and relaxed. "Yeah? Well, how much fuckin' choice a perv got, man? Figure this K-Mart for kids or somethin'?"

Kevin sniffed at him. "You stink, dude. Hate to say it."

Everybody laughed.

"Shut up," said Randers. He looked at Kevin. "Everybody stink, dude. Even you."

"Aw, give him a bath, why don't ya?" said Weasel.

Donny's head came up. He got to his feet and went over to a corner where there was a dirt-crusted deep-sink. The kids all turned to watch as he twisted a rusty faucet. Pipes rattled below and the faucet spat air, followed by a glop of yellow slime, then orange water.

"Never knew that even worked," said Rix.

Randers came over, nodding to Donny. "You a smart dude. Leave it run awhile." He looked back at Whitey.

Whitey gave a sigh, kicking out of his Cheetahs and sliding off his jeans. He waited, naked in the dusty sun. Kevin touched his arm. "You don't got to, man."

Whitey shrugged. "Aw, I ain't ascared of no rusty water."

"He ain't *talkin'* about the water, dipshit," said Randers.

"Yeah? Well, I ain't ascared of no old perv, neither!"

Donny sloshed water around to clean the sink. After a minute the faucet ran clear. He jammed a piece of cardboard in the drain and the sink slowly filled. Whitey walked over, stepping carefully through broken glass, and climbed in. There were snickers and giggles as the other kids gathered until Randers started to look pissed.

Whitey flicked water at everybody. "It ain't bad. It's even warm."

"That 'cause them pipes in the sun," said Donny.

Randers nodded. "Smart dude."

Rix laughed and grabbed Whitey's shoulders. "Dunk him!"

"No!" yelled Whitey.

"Don't forget to get all your dingleberries, man," said Weasel.

"Ain't got no dingleberries like *you,* turd-brain!" said Whitey.

"Shut up," said Randers. "Wash."

Rix pulled the black Iron Maiden T-shirt from around his waist and offered it for a washcloth. Donny found a half-rotted box of Tide on a shelf. After, his huge Def Leppard shirt made a towel. Whitey slipped back into his jeans and Cheetahs.

"He should be wearin' a shirt," said Kevin. "Perv likes to take it off you."

"Why?" asked Whitey.

" 'Cause he does, that's why! Anyways, he won't know you're fat."

"Ain't fat, asshole. Anyways, I didn't bring one today."

Weasel untied his.

"Oh, *too* funny, dude," bawled Whitey.

Randers considered. "Kev. Give him yours. You wear Weasel's."

Kevin's T-shirt, gray and ragged, both sleeves gone, was tight on Whitey and wouldn't cover his stomach all the way. "Keep it sucked in," Randers told him.

"Jeez, I got to fuckin' breathe once in a while, y'know!"

Donny was wringing water from his and Rix's shirts. "I live the closest. I could book home an' get another one of mine."

Kevin glanced at the slanting sun. "Naw. No time. I figure perv's only gonna cruise by once more, wouldn't wanna miss his din-din. After what he done to me he might figure I'm never comin' back an' we'd blow it for sure." He looked at Whitey again. "But you still don't got to do this, man. Really."

"Aw, pervs suck!" said Whitey. " 'Sides, he got no right comin' into our ground, thumpin' on one of us. We don't need no squid dogshit like him just to score some sixers."

Randers clamped a hand on Whitey's shoulder. "You a good dude." He glanced at Kevin. "That perv *always* take you to the old Navy yard?"

"Yeah. Same's he always stops at that Chink-market for the beer."

Rix grinned. "For sure, get the beer!"

Randers picked up a half-full bottle and walked to a window. Five hard-ridden skateboards stood against sooty brick by the sill. Kevin joined him, and they looked down at the street. Randers took a few swallows, then gave the bottle to Kevin. "After we finish this, don't be doin' this perv shit no more, man. It make you old, warp-speed. You not careful, you end like Duncan."

Kevin nodded. "I hear. Only, I wanted to score us stuff, y'know?"

Randers sighed, staring at the street. "I know. We all you friends, man. Friends be for helpin' with shit. Only you makin' a lot of probs lately, especially since you been talkin' to that dealer-puss, Squeaker. Don't wear out you friends, man." He turned around and gazed across the huge empty warehouse to the bayside windows. "Duncan wore out his friends. Even Squeaker couldn't use him no more then."

Randers picked up his board, a battered Chris Miller, and fingered the tail, ground sharp behind the skid. Among the stickers on the downside was one that read, "When your board is your only weapon, USE IT!"

Kevin put down the bottle and snagged his own board, an Alva. Whitey came over and got his thrashed old Steve Steadham, then walked toward the stairwell. Kevin started after him, but Randers took his arm. "Wait. I be tellin' you, dude, straight up. You wearin' people lately. Max. You play with you own ass, that cool. But Whitey puttin' his out for you now. Remember that!"

"Yeah."

"Okay," said Randers. "We be there. Full-on!"

Kevin thought a minute. "For me . . . or Whitey?"

"Both of you. Dumb-ass question, man."

Out on the sidewalk, Whitey asked, "How many times you go with this perv, anyways?"

Kevin dropped his board, and decked. "Six or seven. First times were no prob, just ran the same old perv-shit games, like I'm just another dumb-ass squid-kid, like in Silicone-land. They must gots some really stupid kids there, man. Y'know? Get the kid all wasted then try an' play touchy-feely? Shit! *He* acted more like a kid than that stupid Russel who's only eight. It was okay though, kept buyin' all the beer I wanted. . . . " He glanced back at Whitey. "Never heard none of you dudes bitchin' about that!"

They rolled along the buckled sidewalk, wheels clicking cracks.

"Well," said Whitey. "Nobody bitches about scorin' beer."

70

Kevin shrugged. "Yeah. I noticed, man. Anyways, the last couple times he starts into drinkin' too, a lot. Might've been doin' it before he got here even. Starts tellin' me all his probs, he makes computers or somethin' I think. Even tells me about his old-lady an' kids."

"Um, how come he don't do this shit on his own kids?"

"They don't treat kids that way in Silicone-land."

"Oh."

"Anyways, sounds like one of 'em's a retard or somethin', don't do very good at school, dropped outa boy scouts. Shit! My heart pumps peanut-butter for him, man." Kevin grinned and turned half-around. "Here's this old dude—gots himself a Beamer with a Blaupunkt—an' he's tellin *me* his probs. Sometimes it's hard to keep from crackin' up, man!"

Whitey cut around a sewer cover. "So? What happen after that?"

"Aw, he starts into bitchin' about havin' to buy them extra sixers, the ones I bring back for all of us. Like *he* can't afford 'em, like I'm supposed to be his friend now or somethin'. Last time I told him, hey, you play, you pay, duuude!"

"Yeah? Then what?"

"He beats the fuckin' shit outa me, that's what! Keeps screamin' he don't take that shit from his own kids, so he's for sure not gonna from a dirty little animal like me." Kevin laughed. "Dig on it, man. That's what he called me—a *animal!*"

Whitey giggled. "Synchronicity."

"Or what! Anyways, he almost broke my nose. Then he starts chokin' me. I figured I was history, dude."

"Jeez!"

Kevin caught some air over an alley curb. "Yeah. But then, after, he gives me all this 'I'm sorry' dogshit. Bought them two twelvers the dudes thought were so hot, an' rides me back to Donny's like it's all cool again an' I'm gonna forget he just tried to off me. Asshole must figure kids don't remember that kinda stuff or somethin'."

Kevin jumped a gutter and slapped the opposite curb, worn ribs grinding up and over. He didn't have a lapper and the rear truck hung a second but he kicked the nose down and rolled on.

"Maybe them Silicone kids *don't* remember very long when bad stuff happens," said Whitey. He lost it on the curb, but scrambled up and decked again.

Kevin grinned back at him. "Maybe. Or they're just too scared to do nuthin' about it. Shit! I even got back at him a little that time, man. Got my blood all over his stupid Beamer."

"Yeah," said Whitey. "That might bum somebody like that."

"That's what I figured too. I rolled around a lot. Anyways, out front of Donny's he tells me he's bored! Wanted to know if I knew any 'black boys.' When I finally said I did, you wouldn't *believe* some of the shit he asked."

Whitey kicked closer. "Yeah? Like?"

"Aw, don't even ask, man. You might get your feelin's hurt. It was weird. Believe it!"

"C'mon, tell me some of it."

"Naw. It's really dumb. Anyways, he wanted to know if I had any black friends who dug doin' shit like that."

"Yeah? Like what? Gettin' your ass wiped, sounds like."

"Naw. He ain't gonna hurt you." Kevin thought a minute, then rolled nearer to Whitey. "Know what? I figure he's really ascared of black kids."

"Yeah? Well, he should be ascared of *any* kids, man! Totally!" Whitey yanked the tight T-shirt down over his stomach again. "You figure he even want me?"

"Just act real stupid, like Beaver."

"Sound like he like little kids, anyways."

"Naw. I don't figure them kind of dudes like kids at all, man. Even their own. They're just scared of gettin' caught doin' somethin' like that at home."

Whitey considered. "Yeah? Well, that Alpo dude at the center be a homo, an' he likes kids, you can tell. He tries to be cool, even if he don't know how to be. I mean, he never tries to touch you or nuthin', not even Eric, an' you know how Eric looks—almost pretty like a girl? But anyways, Alpo's okay. Nobody likes him much 'cause he a homo, but he still okay."

"Aw, he's a homo like you said, but not a perv. He gets off with dudes as old as him. Hey, like your big brother wanna mess with a little girl?"

"No way!"

"Well, that's like what I mean."

They rolled a little further up the block then tailed in front of a bar. Stale beer-smell and cigarette smoke drifted from the open door. Bruce Springsteen moaned from the jukebox, and sometimes somebody would laugh inside or ice would tinkle against glass. Kevin and Whitey sat on the curb, standing their boards against a fireplug that dripped. Kevin pointed to it. "You're all sweaty again. Take off your shirt and wash under your arms at least."

"Hey! I don't smell bad."

"Not to me. Only, the perv figures . . . "

"What?"

"Aw, nuthin', man! This is serious! You wanna thrash that perv or not?"

"Fuck! It wasn't me . . . "

"What?"

Whitey shrugged. "Nuthin'." He pulled off his shirt and splashed some water around. Then they sat back against the plug, knees up. Kevin had two Marlboros left and they smoked, not talking.

Kevin just finished his cigarette when he caught a glint of metallic blue up the block. "Perv comin', dude. When you get in his car, keep your board where you can snag it fast! Hey, an' when you stand up now . . . "

"I know, asshole. Suck in my fuckin' tum Jeez!"

"Yeah. An' you're Mikey, okay?"

"Mikey?"

"Yeah. An' I told the perv my name was Timmy."

"This's dogshit, man. Weirdorama to the max."

"He's comin'! Shut up! Make sure an' score the beer *first!* I'll be with the other dudes. You'll be okay, man. We won't let nuthin' happen to you."

"Aw, I know, man." Whitey smiled. "I get killed or somethin', you howl over my grave, skate on my stone."

Kevin gave him a quick kid-shake. "Believe it, dude!"

There was a nervous whine from a fast-idling engine, and the Beamer was beside them. Kevin knew it had AC, but the dude inside was shirtless, pale, and chubby like a kid himself, almost. He wore his mirror sunglasses—probably figured to make him look bad, Kevin thought. The dude checked the street, both ways, then the passenger window slid down with a sigh. "Hi, Timmy."

Both kids stood. Whitey kept his belly tight. Kevin smiled at the dude. "Um, this's my friend, Mikey."

Whitey shuffled his dirty Cheetahs and smiled too.

"That's Jim, Mikey," Kevin said.

Jim checked the street again. Kevin figured he probably thought he was being cool, but any cop car around would've been there warp-speed.

Jim studied Whitey. "Mikey's kind of big."

Kevin looked at the gutter, rolling his hands up in the front of his shirt, like little kids did when confused. "Um, he's my best friend of all, Jim. Um, he's like you said, y'know? About black boys?"

Jim seemed to chew on his lip a little. "You mean, you two . . . do things?"

"Sure," said Kevin. "All the time."

Whitey wasn't dense. He frowned a little. Jim looked at Whitey again. "You want to cruise, blood?"

Whitey shot Kevin a glance, then nodded. "Yeah. That'd be . . . neat, mister."

Jim popped the door. "Hey, call me Jim, little guy. Let's be friends, okay?"

Whitey climbed in with his board. Kevin gave him a quick pat on the arm. The nervous engine whined again and the Beamer jerked away with a squeak of rubber. Kevin waited a minute then slammed down his board and ripped along the sidewalk. His wheels were good old Kryptonic 70s and all the Animals had Tri-Flowed their bearings that morning. It was about a mile along the water to the old Navy yard, but Kevin figured he had plenty of time if the perv stopped at the market as usual for beer. He caught air back over the curb, slapping onto the other side, crouched low and went for it hard. He burned past the old warehouse where they'd first watched the Beamer and glanced up at the third-floor windows. Donny might still be there; he was too fat to ride, but the broken windows grinned down—empty, black-holes in the late sunlight.

The other Animals were for sure already at the yard by now. Fresh paint scraped on the next curb, metallic purple off Weasel's old ribless Variflex, show'd they'd gone. A couple of blocks ahead Kevin saw the Beamer pull left in front of the little market. He made a fast kick-turn into a doorway and tailed, knocking a wine bottle skittering, waiting, head poked around the corner, watching as the perv went in. Then he decked and rolled again, fast, shooting past the Beamer on the opposite side of the street.

In the car, Whitey looked out and raised a thumb, even giving Kevin a small grin. He had the perv's Blaupunkt maxed, KSOL, it sounded like—hard rap music in the hot salty air.

At the next block, Kevin cut across and up a side street, staying in the middle where the crumbling asphalt was still smoothest; then right at the next corner, along a row of junk cars and parked semi-trailers. There was a narrow sidewalk, cracked and littered with trash, but better than the potholed pavement. He crouched, cutting under a trailer, just missing the spare-tire rack, and onto concrete again. The last curb showed more purple paint. Weasel needed ribs, bad.

The street dead-ended in dry weeds and garbage and a rusty chain-link fence with sagging barbed wire on top. A faded sign read, "U.S. Government Property—KEEP OUT." Kevin tailed, threw his board over, and climbed the fence where the wire was already broken. Inside was gravel and more dry weeds rusting uneasily in the faint breeze. Kevin glanced around. Somewhere a seagull cried, but the only other sounds were the distant traffic drone from 880. He snagged his board and ran toward a line of old concrete buildings.

"Yo, Kev!"

Randers leaned from a broken window. Kevin darted over, throwing his board. Randers caught it and helped Kevin scramble up. Sweaty kid smell surrounded Kevin, familiar and good.

The building was huge and dark, empty except for some splintered pallet on the dusty floor. The kids walked across to where reddish evening light stabbed through cracks in a big, wooden door. Randers slid the door back a few inches, rusted rollers squealing on their track, and the Animals crowded the opening. Out front was a long roof over broken weedy concrete, held up by iron posts.

"This the place?" asked Randers.

Kevin nodded. "Always." He pointed to a post with a lot of Bud and Heinie bottles scattered around it. "Perv sucks the Heinie, kid gets the Bud."

"Pervs suck anyways," giggled Weasel. "Hey, how come you can't get lost in San Francisco?"

"Shut up," said Randers.

" 'Cause there's AIDS on every corner," whispered Rix.

Randers spun around but there was engine-sound from the distant street. The kids pushed toward the opening again, watching the Beamer cut between torn gates, tires crunching gravel as it came toward the line of buildings. The kids pressed closer. Randers shoved them back. "*Wait,* assholes!"

Rix touched Kevin's shoulder. "Jeez, man, you shakin'."

"Fuck off."

"Shut up," Randers hissed.

Across the Bay, the sun dropped below the jagged skyline. The iron posts threw long shadows as the Beamer wove between and stopped by the bottles. Its windows were down and Kevin saw Whitey's arms go up as the perv pulled his shirt off. The engine cut and they heard Whitey giggle above the stereo, "Hey, dude . . . "

Randers shoved the door open. "Book!"

Boards slapped concrete. Wheels snapped across cracks, glass and gravel spitting from under them. The Beamer's passenger door flew open and Whitey was out and decked in seconds. He jerked up his zipper and cut back with the other Animals as they circled the car.

The perv could have booked easy, Kevin thought. But he kicked open his door and jumped out instead, staring over the roof at Whitey. "Get back here, you fucking little nigger."

The perv left his door open and took a few steps, each slower than the last as he looked around at the kids. It was getting hard to see in the fading light. Finally he stopped and just stood, watching, looking a little confused as the Animals circled and the dusk deepened.

It was time, Kevin thought, knowing the other kids knew it too. Randers had told them once that second warnings were only for movies. Kevin rolled past the post, crouching on his board, and grabbing up a bottle. He smiled. The perv could still book if he jammed for his car fast enough. But he wouldn't. Where he came from nobody was afraid of kids.

The other Animals cut past the bottles, each snagging one. Randers scooped up two but his hands were a little bigger. Randers rolled straight at the perv, tailing about twenty feet from him. The others stopped alongside. They stood for awhile, together and silent, each with a foot on his board, boards erect like Cobras. Their small kid-shadows stretched out toward the man.

Still, the man just stood. Kevin studied him. He looked like just a big kid now—a big chubby stupid boy. It was getting hard to see his face.

The man shifted a little, glancing back at his car. Then he faced the Animals again. "Fuck you!" he yelled. "You're nothing but a bunch of dirty little kids."

Kevin threw the first bottle.

There were plenty of bottles. It didn't last long.

The last light faded out across the Bay as the kids came close and stood over the man. He was almost back in his car, but on the ground, face hidden behind his arm. Randers spit on him. "You *ever* come back here, you *dead!* Hear me?"

Weasel had his arm over Whitey's shoulders. He grinned and leaned forward. "Yeah, an' you can tell everybody back in Silicone-land that a bunch of dirty little kids done this too."

Rix snickered. *"Nigger kids."*

"Skate-punks," added Whitey.

Randers bent closer to the man. "You hear? Answer me, cock-sucker!"

The man nodded, still hiding his face. Kevin wasn't sure but the dude could've been crying. Kevin stepped forward and leaned on the door. "An' hey, my name ain't Timmy, just like yours ain't Jim. An' kids ain't as stupid as you figure, asshole." He spat then jerked back his leg to kick but Randers took his arm.

"Naw, dude. You only get your Nike all dirty."

Randers looked around at the others. "Leave him one light. He got a long drive home. Maybe he think."

The kids thrashed the car. The man stayed where he was.

Finally, Whitey snagged the two sixers out of the glass on the back seat. Weasel took one, then the Animals decked and rolled into the darkness. Kevin stopped and looked back.

"Don't take it out on your kids, man."

Fire

"HEAR ME, you little dipshit. Fuck-off... *now!*"

Randers stood, legs apart, hands on narrow hips, and pissed as hell. The other Animals, sitting on the dumpster behind him, grinned and nudged each other. A little boy gazed up at Randers. He was about eight, and white, though summer tanned almost as dark as Randers because he hardly ever wore a shirt, and his small kid-muscles had the same hard definition as the older boy's. His hair was long and black over his shoulders and, like the Animals, he wore a big dog choker around his neck. He had ragged jeans with one knee gone, one black riot glove with rusty studs, and a punker-kid cap on backwards. His huge hightop Nikes looked like moon boots. He held a thrashed old Variflex skateboard and had that stupid-sullen look little kids got when they were scared shitless and trying not to let it show.

The Animals on the dumpster smoked and grinned and waited. Randers glared down at the kid, and the kid kept his eyes on Randers' sweaty chest and didn't move.

Randers gave a small shrug and hit the boy hard. The kid slammed back against a brick wall and slid down on his little ass. He shook his head and blinked tears away. Blood ran down his chin.

Randers dropped his hands and looked at the kid. On the dumpster, Weasel blew smoke and leaned forward, amber eyes peering from under his pale shaggy mop. His face, normally open and friendly, looked a little sad now. "Go home, Russel," he called to the boy.

"Shut up, man," said Randers.

Russel got slowly up from garbage. His eyes were wet and shiny and blood dripped down his chest. He took one step forward and looked at Randers again. He took a breath. "I wanna be a Animal."

Rix squirmed on the hot dumpster lid, his long wiry body gleaming ebony with sweat. Though the same age as the others, he was easily a head and a half taller. "Chill out, Russel," he said softly. "Go home."

Beside Rix, Kevin said, "Aw, wannabe, or what."

Russel didn't move, and grins faded, except for Kevin. He leaned forward, tangled mongrel-blond hair almost hiding cold blue eyes. The cigarette in his fingers was rolled sloppily from Bugler tobacco and everybody smelled the rock in it.

"Shut up," Randers said again. He might've sighed when he hit Russel this time.

The kid's head thunked brick and it was a few seconds before his eyes opened and cleared.

"You get up, I only hit you again, dude," Randers warned.

The other Animals stared down at the broken concrete, except Kevin.

"Aw, he *can't* get up again," Kevin said. "Hey, Russel, I hear the Rats are lookin' for a butt-boy."

Russel's green eyes burned fierce.

"Shut the fuck up!" Randers bawled.

Mid-morning sun blasted down between the buildings, and the alley already baked in tar and rotting-garbage smell. Exhaust stink drifted in from the street and the dumpster lids sent up shimmering waves of heat. But the Animals all sat quietly and dripped sweat. Rix's old blaster played low and scratchy on dying batteries.

"Slam him in the stomach next time," Kevin suggested.

Randers spun around and grabbed Kevin's thin shoulders, yanking him down so that their foreheads cracked together. Eyes locked. "You gettin' strange, man," Randers said, voice tense and husky. "Really, really strange . . . like Duncan, just afore he go an' off hisself."

On the other side of Kevin, Whitey shrugged and offered a smile. "Well, shit. You be strange too, doin' all that rock."

"Shut up, man," said Randers.

"Aw, Duncan was *old*," said Kevin. "Fuck. He was almost fifteen, just couldn't handle shit no more." He smiled a little at Randers. " 'Sides, he was a puss anyways."

Randers dropped his hands. "Dude wipe *your* ass enough times."

Kevin leaned back and shrugged, taking a long hit off his cigarette and holding smoke. "Yeah? An' what the fuck good that do him? He's dead—*for*-ever—an' I'm still here."

Randers turned away, his forehead creased. "Yeah," he said. "Yeah."

Russel got up, but kept his face lowered. He snagged his board and dragged it behind him down the alley.

Weasel watched. "That's a hard little dude, man."

Randers looked at the blood drops drying on hot concrete. "Yeah."

"You do this kinda stuff in Fresno?" Donny asked, pointing to the sidewalk where an "A" was scratched faint and fresh.

Robby looked at it, then to the alley mouth. "Sometimes." He glanced back at Donny. "Figure you Animals gonna kick my ass?"

Donny shrugged. "Well, you don't gotta come." He pointed up the street. "Bus station's that way. You said you still gots your ticket." He grinned. "You could just go on 'cross the water, see your ocean."

Robby grinned too. "Yeah, right. Um, thanks for tellin' me about that. I was pretty stupid, huh? No wonder that dude in the van looked at me funny."

Donny cocked his head. "What dude?"

Robby shrugged. "Aw, nuthin'." He turned and gazed out at the Bay. "I'll see the real ocean, man. Someday before I die."

Donny considered. " 'Course, we could always go back up to the

Center. I could show you to Nathaniel. He figure somethin' about you."

"You mean the dude with the food? He sure didn't look like your drawin'."

Donny made a face. "That wasn't Nathaniel, dipshit. That's Alpo. He's okay, 'cept he don't know his ass from his elbow."

Robby shook his head. "Naw. Nathaniel'd only send me back to Fresno, man."

"No he wouldn't! Not if you didn't wanna go."

Robby looked doubtful. "Aw, get real. What else could he do? You just can't keep a kid around like a dog or somethin'."

Donny crossed his arms over his chest and looked stubborn. "Well, he wouldn't send you back if you didn't wanna go. Believe it!"

Robby shrugged. "So it's kick my ass time, huh? Can you say that? For sure you can."

Donny smiled and looked toward the alley. "I never say you was gonna get your ass wiped for sure, dipshit. Hard to figure just what Randers gonna do sometimes. Hell, you look so much like Whitey, he might think that funny. " 'Course, he still might wipe your ass anyhow, but he ain't gonna kill you or nuthin'."

"Oh well, that's cool enough I guess. Shit, I been beat up so many times, man."

Donny grinned. "Aw, quit braggin'."

There was the sound of wood dragging concrete as Russel came around a dumpster.

"Jeez!" Robby muttered.

Donny smiled. "Aw, it his own fault. He keep tryin' to hang with us an' he just too stupid to be ascared of nuthin'. He might even be a retard." Donny turned to the boy. "You cool, Russel?"

Russel gave his eyes a savage wipe. "Randers call me *'dude'!*"

Donny grinned at Robby. Russel puffed his little chest, decked, and rolled.

"Jeez, them trucks are loose," Robby said, watching Russel. "Good thing he don't weigh nuthin' or his wheels would rub on every corner." He looked down at the blood. "Hell, why don't he wipe his face at least?"

"Aw, now he ride to the Center an' show all the other little dudes how Randers wipe his ass. Still wanna come? Randers could do that to you just as easy."

"Like I said, that wouldn't be nuthin' new. 'Sides, we had a little kid trying' to hang with us all the time too. How else you gonna get 'em to leave?" Robby dabbed at a blood spot with his toe. "Um, 'case I do get killed or somethin', thanks for lettin' me stay at your place last night."

"No prob, man. Gets kinda lonely sometimes."

"Well, if you'd lose some weight, maybe you could learn to ride like the other dudes?"

Donny grinned and slapped his belly. "Yeah, right. Maybe in ten fuckin' years! I'm a Animal anyways an' that's plenty good enough." He started up the alley. "C'mon then, dude. Like the sticker say, Don't die wonderin'."

Rix tuned his blaster but the batteries were almost dead and it wouldn't go any louder. "I can't hang all day," he said to Randers. "My mom wants to take me up an' score some new school clothes."

"Aw, don't *even* talk about that dogshit, man," said Weasel. "I got Mrs. Martin this year. Mega-bitch Martin!"

There were footsteps, and Randers spun around, the others all looking up as Donny led Robby around a dumpster. Randers gave Rix a narrow-eyed glance. "You 'sposed to be watchin', asshole. Not fuckin' with you goddamn boomer!"

"Um, sorry."

"Sorry, my ass! You wanna get dead *for*-ever? It happen that way."

Like Donny, Robby had his shirt off and was already sweating in the baking alley air. He carried his board by one wheel, downside in, and saw the five other boards leaning against a wall, all good ones, all ridden hard. He remembered Donny's drawing and there was no problem figuring out which Animal was which. Weasel even looked a little friendlier, but Kevin looked a lot badder. Randers just looked pissed.

"Yo, Donny," Kevin called.

Randers gave Kevin a look, but Kevin didn't notice. Whitey

punched Kevin's shoulder and shrugged at Randers. "He out of it, man."

Randers spat on the concrete. "No shit! Just keep him shut up!" He walked towards Robby.

"Um, this is Robby," said Donny. "He's cool."

Randers ignored Donny and stopped in front of Robby. "Who the fuck are you?"

"Robby," said Robby.

Kevin snickered. "Yeah? He looks more like Whitey's twin, man, only Whitey's fatter."

Whitey shoved him. "Ain't fat, asshole!"

Randers twisted half around. "One more motherfuckin' *word.*" He turned back to Robby and took his board. Robby let it go. Randers flipped it, glanced at the stickers, then tossed it over his shoulder. Weasel caught it, and the others checked it out. "Steadham," said Rix. "Jus' like yours, Whitey. Synchronicity."

"Shhh!" hissed Weasel.

"Why you here?" asked Randers.

"He run away," said Donny.

"I run away," said Robby.

"From where?" Randers gave Donny a look.

"Fresno," said Robby.

"Where that?"

Robby shrugged. "A real long ways."

"Why?"

"Everythin' sucked, man. They was gonna stick me in a foster home."

"Shit," said Weasel. "That ain't nuthin'. I'm in one."

"Shut up!" said Randers. "How you come here?"

"On a bus."

Rix whispered to Weasel, "Um, what you figure Randers gonna do?"

Weasel shrugged. "I don't know. This kinda shit never happened before. Ain't like he was from here an' come into our ground on purpose, y'know? Then we could just wipe his ass, no prob. Dude come all that way, got no home, don't seem right."

Whitey leaned over. "Yeah? Big deal. Kevin almost don't got no home no more."

Weasel turned to him. "Yeah, but that's different, man. He's got one, he just can't go there 'cause his mom gots customers all the time."

"Fresno in L.A.?" asked Rix.

Weasel shrugged. "Maybe."

Whitey pointed to the Skully Brothers sticker on Robby's board. "I think I seen that in *Thrasher*."

Rix nodded. "Yeah, me too. Looks pretty hot, huh?"

"Aw, just wipe the fucker's ass!" yelled Kevin.

Whitey glanced at Weasel. "Well, you wanna do it?"

"Naw. Go ahead."

Whitey hit Kevin hard in the stomach, then slammed him back on the dumpster lid, scrambling on top and holding him down. Kevin fought. "It's burnin' me, fucker!"

Randers gave Robby a long look. "I get back to you, man." He twisted around. "Leave him go!"

Whitey rolled off and Randers grabbed Kevin's leg, yanking him flat on the concrete. Kevin's head hit with a thud and he halfway struggled up. Randers' hand was open as he hit Kevin across the face and the sound made Robby wince. Randers slammed Kevin back against the dumpster, grabbing his shoulders and shaking him hard. "Got no *time* for this shit. Hear me!"

Kevin looked sullen and nodded, wiping his mouth.

Randers stood and sighed, then glanced at Weasel. "Gimme a smoke, man."

Weasel held out his Marlboro pack and Whitey fired his Bic. Rix tapped Robby's board with a finger. "Aw, maybe he can't even ride, man?"

Randers sucked a big lungful of smoke, letting it out slow and looking disgusted. "Pull my hose, asshole. Figure this showtime or somethin'? *Look* at the fuckin' thing, dipshit! It fit him. Dude couldn't ride it, dude wouldn't got it!" He snatched the board and flung it back to Robby, then glanced at his knuckles, bloody from Russel's teeth. He walked up to Robby, jamming his fist under Robby's nose, smearing blood on his lip. "What that smell?"

Robby didn't move. "You, man."

"See? I told you he was cool," Donny said.

Randers thought a moment, then nodded. "Mmmm. Yeah. You remember me, dude, till I say you stop." He turned to Donny. "Take him somewhere, man . . . away from me. Show him this dogshit place. Maybe he figure Fresno pretty hot after all. Hell, take him to the Center, leastways he get fed. Maybe Nathaniel wanna see some runaway dipshit. We gots probs today, man. Got no time for strange stuff now."

Down the alley, a beer can crunched as a car turned in. The Animals all tensed, Robby too. He shot a glance up the other way where the street showed clear, and noted a rusty fire ladder leading to a roof. Rap music echoed between the sooty walls. "Oakland, California, the city of light . . . "

Weasel made a face. "An' there's the probs, man."

"Shut up," said Randers.

Robby listened a minute, then whispered to Donny, "That's some bad rap."

Donny nodded. "Or what. That's Too Short. Don't get much badder."

"Shut up," said Randers. He glanced at Robby. "You stay. Maybe you see somethin' now make you wish you back in Fresno, warpspeed!" He flipped his cigarette away as a black 'Vette wove between the dumpsters and garbage cans. It was spotless, with chrome centerlines shimmering in the sun. A black kid was driving and another, younger, sat beside him.

Kevin climbed stiffly back on the dumpster, wiping at his mouth. Donny jerked his head at Robby and they moved against it too. Randers kicked over a garbage can and sat. All watched as the 'Vette rolled up, engine like low thunder.

"Yo, Rander-man," the driver-kid called. He was shirtless, with long Michael J. hair, and clean.

Randers yawned and glanced at Weasel. "You hear somethin', man?"

Weasel scratched his bushy mop. "Thought I heard a dog fart."

The driver-kid grinned, cutting the engine and stereo. Def Leppard still came soft from Rix's blaster.

"Got somethin' to say," said the driver-kid.

Randers spat between his ragged Cheetahs. "Yeah? What the matter, Squeaker? Don't you puss-car door open?"

Squeaker grinned again and slid out. Robby studied him. He wore clean new jeans, like the kind you saw at the mall, huge Adidas that'd never seen sidewalk, and a big studded belt. He had a heavy chain around his neck, one on his left ankle, and a massive earring. All glittered gold in the sun. He had some muscles but his stomach was soft and beginning to hang over his belt buckle.

The younger kid was out in a second too. He looked about thirteen, though his body was all what Robby's mom would call baby fat. He was dressed about like Squeaker and carried a totally badass-looking gun. Robby'd seen an M-16 once, but this gun looked a lot badder, even with the Corey O'Brien flying death stickers on it. The gun-kid scowled, which, Robby thought, wasn't easy for his baby-face, and clicked a little switch on the gun, resting the muzzle on one shoulder.

Squeaker checked the Animals, calling by name until he saw Robby.

"Robby," said Robby, voice flat.

Squeaker smiled at him and nodded. He was a pretty cool-looking dude, Robby thought, honey-brown, small snub nose, and bright black eyes with long soft lashes. Of course, the new clothes, gold, and clean bod helped a lot too.

Squeaker looked back at Randers. "Got yourself some bad homeys, Rander-man."

Randers spat again. "Don't be comin' down here with you homeboy dogshit, playin' that tape all them white-boys score for to look bad! Take you act back over East where they got all them show an' tell pusses!"

Squeaker's eyes narrowed. "Yeah? Well, what is, *is* sometimes, man. Show *and* tell!"

Randers laughed. "I got eyes, man. All they see is the show!"

Squeaker snapped his fingers and the gun-kid came around, digging a flat white box from his pocket. Robby watched. The box said

"Shermans" on it, and that made him think of tanks on TV. He also saw the black gun was getting sun-hot and the kid shifted it from hand to hand, almost looking like he wished he could put it down. Robby studied the gun, pretending not to. It looked new, but all guns looked new, except up really close. But he noticed the part behind the trigger had electric tape wrapped around it like something was broken.

Squeaker flashed the box at Randers and flipped the lid. Robby's nose wrinkled a little—nothing but homo-looking cigarettes.

"Want a smoke, dude?" Squeaker asked.

"Naw. Them say queen-size, man. Where you score 'em, 'cross the water on Castro Street?"

Weasel giggled and held down his Marlboro pack. Randers took one and Whitey was ready with his Bic. Randers blew smoke while the gun-kid fumbled out a gold lighter and fired for Squeaker.

"Randers *never* gots to snap his fingers, man," snickered Weasel.

Robby started to smile. Then he noticed that Kevin was checking everything about Squeaker to the max.

"Hey, man," Rix called to the gun-kid. "Didn't you used to be Calvin?"

The gun-kid made a face and spat.

"That T.C., man," said Squeaker.

"Too Cute?" Robby asked, before he could think about it.

Randers glanced at him, one eyebrow slightly raised. Rix's lips parted over big buck teeth. Weasel and Whitey giggled. Even Kevin smiled a little. T.C. thumbed the switch again. Robby could see tiny white letters, A.F.S. The switch was on A now.

Squeaker blew smoke and smiled with his mouth. "Too funny, Robman." He put his hands on his hips and looked around again. "Yeah! Some baaad dudes here for sure. Hey, Randers, how much buck you got in them raggedy-ass jeans?"

Randers shrugged. "Enough."

"Yeah? For a sixer of dog-piss? How'd you like Heinie, man? Every fuckin' day?"

"So he get a beer-belly like you?" Weasel asked.

Squeaker frowned at Randers and spread his hands. "Seem like your dudes don't respect you much, man. You are still doin' the talkin', ain't ya?"

"What it is," said Randers, "be like bad dudes be hard to con-trol, y'know? Sorta like 'tack dogs." He smiled up at Squeaker. "Leastways I don't gotta change they Pampers."

T.C. scowled again and fingered his gun.

"Hey, man," said Squeaker. "It could be snowin' all over you dudes like Christmas or somethin'."

Donny nudged Robby and whispered, "It snow in Fresno, man?"

"Only his kind."

"Oh."

"It snow all over Duncan, man," said Randers. "Make him cold . . . *for*-ever."

Squeaker shrugged. "Duncan couldn't handle it, man. What can I say?"

"Yeah? Seem like nobody handle it long." Randers gave Squeaker a sudden smile. "Even you, man! We gots ears, too. We hear about East. Seem big dudes there gettin' kinda pissed over show-boy like you." He yawned and stretched. "Hell, can't nobody tell if you a real dealer or just cruisin' around sellin' you boy's chubby little ass."

Squeaker's smile faded. T.C. shifted his hot gun. Both were starting to sweat just like the Animals.

Randers grinned. "Yeah! What the matter . . . boy? You comin' down here 'cause soon you be leavin' East, warp-speed?" Randers stood up. Squeaker was taller, but for a second it didn't look that way to Robby.

Randers dropped his hands to his hips. Squeaker might've sucked in his stomach. Randers didn't have to. "Hey," said Randers. "Maybe you get old enough for a fuckin' learner permit, you can cruise you puss-car over the Bridge. Take you dogshit 'cross the water. Dis-turb some shit over there." He spat at Squeaker's feet. "Better be takin' twenty papers, boy! You gonna need new seat covers, or what!"

The Animals snickered and giggled. T.C. shifted his gun and watched Squeaker. Randers spat again, just missing Squeaker's Adidas. "Do a homo an' blow, boy. We not want to play today."

Squeaker spat at Randers' feet. "Yeah? Yeah? You gots nuthin', boy! Total, total zip!" He stabbed a finger toward the row of boards. "You just dirty smelly little kids with toys. Shredders, my ass! What you got? Three shitty blocks 'cause nobody else stupid enough to *even* want 'em. Hey, skate-punk nigger-boy! Dude come with fire, what you do? Throw dogshit? I from here, remember, boy? I know!"

Donny stepped forward. "Yeah? Tell it to Duncan, man. Tell it to the Rats!" For a moment Donny didn't look like a fat kid—just a big kid. Squeaker almost stepped back. Then he smiled again and looked up at Kevin. "*There* a smart white-boy. Hey, smart white-boy, you tired of bein' dogshit with these niggers?"

Kevin said nothing.

Weasel yanked his tattered T-shirt from around his waist and held it up for Squeaker to see. Squeaker ignored him and pulled a rock bottle out of his pocket. He tossed it to Kevin. "You think, dude." He glanced around at the other kids. "All you dudes think. Nobody got time for dirty dogshit kids, black or white . . . special when they got no buck."

Squeaker got back in the car. T.C. waited for him to start the engine then slid in too. Squeaker revved once, loud, and the black 'Vette rolled. The Animals watched until it turned into the street.

"Squeaker must got two-by-fours taped on them pedals," Whitey snickered.

"Naw," said Weasel. "T.C. pushes 'em. Squeaker just steers an' tries to look bad."

"We call 'em low-riders in Fresno," said Robby.

Randers glanced at him while the others laughed. "You got *him* in Fresno?"

"For sure. Except he drives this Nissan four-by-four, all shiny silver, an' gots a Chicano T.C. with a sawed-off twelver."

Randers thought a minute. "You can hang if you want, dude. We gonna score us some beer."

Rix giggled. "Hey, Rob-man. Too Cute. Too funny! I'm Rix."

The others said their names and Robby nodded like he didn't already know.

Rix slid off the dumpster and knelt beside his blaster. The batteries were dead. "Hey, Robby, can you rap?"

Robby shrugged, moving close to the other boys. "Sometimes, when I'm drunk."

Kevin studied Robby. Finally he smiled. "Yeah? That's about like Rix, man. Fuck! Weasel can rap better'n him!"

"Or what," snickered Weasel. "An' I'm just a . . . " He held up his shirt again.

"Aw, pull my hose!" muttered Rix.

Whitey leaned down and thumped Rix's head. "So? Do the one about Weasel."

Rix looked shy. "Aw. . . . "

"Yeah! Do it, man," said Donny. "Robby never heard it." He started to clap and the others joined.

Rix gave Robby a shy grin. "All you homeys gonna listen to my rap, 'bout a dude name Weasel who's sister got the clap. . . . "

"I don't really got no sister," Weasel said to Robby. "But it fits better."

"Shut up," said Randers, smiling.

> *. . . this dude hangin' home on a hot summer day,*
> *an' he bored as hell 'cause there ain't no way,*
> *for a kid got nuthin' in this motherfuckin' city,*
> *to have no fun at all an' that a God damn pity.*
> *Cocaine cos' an' it gone too fast,*
> *an' the cracker fuck your brain an'*
> *leave you dyin' on your ass.*
> *Shoulder-tappin' for some beer sure do get to be a drag,*
> *an' you end up pukin' or molested by a fag.*
> *Doin' acid's for the freaks,*
> *doin' dust be for the squids,*
> *seem there no kinda nuthin' for a poor city kid.*
> *So he do a little doober but that only make him cry,*
> *'cause he sad an' lonely*
> *an' just wishin' he could die.*
> *Everybody give him shit, ain't nobody give him lovin',*
> *so he go an' stick a rat in a microwave oven.*

Now what happens to ole rat just don't gotta be explain',
so now everybody know just how Weasel get his name.

"Yeah!" yelled Whitey. "All right, duuude! I like that one the best."

Kevin poked Weasel. "Now you do the one about Rix an' the Thundercats."

Randers shook his head. "Naw, dudes. Got no time. We gotta score some Bud today, remember?"

Rix looked at Randers. "I gotta book anyways, man. My mom be pissed."

Randers had turned and was gazing up the alley where the 'Vette had gone. "Yeah. Later, dude. We save you some."

Kevin slipped the rock bottle into his pocket and looked at Randers. "What'er you thinkin', man?"

Randers stared up the empty alley. "That Squeaker always full of dogshit. Even when I in third grade an' he in four, I could easy wipe his ass. Dude say one thing . . . "

"Yeah?"

"Animals got no fire like he."

"Figure we're gonna need it?" asked Weasel.

Randers nodded. "Or what. An' soon."

Rix snagged his board and blaster. "Well, I hope all the shootin' get done before school start."

Weasel stuck his finger down his throat and crossed his eyes. Whitey covered his ears. "School! Fuck off, dude!"

Rix grinned, decked, and rolled.

Donny raised a thumb at Rix, then moved over by Randers. "Um, how you know about Squeaker havin' probs over East, man?"

Randers shrugged, smiling slightly. "I make it up."

"Um," said Robby, moving close too. "Sure the hell freaked him."

"Nobody says 'freaked' anymore," said Kevin. " 'Cept old hippies."

"Oh. Thanks."

Randers considered. "Figure it true. No other way Squeaker be gettin' hot an' bothered over this dogshit place we got."

Weasel leaned forward. "Hey, Randers. You got the .44 mag, an' Donny gots the Army gun. Squeaker don't know about them."

Randers gave Weasel a frown, flicking his eyes toward Robby.

"Um," said Donny. "He knows, man. I told him last night. He's cool."

Randers studied Robby for a minute or two. "Yeah."

"Well, T.C. gots the Uzi," said Kevin. "Fuck, we'd be better off throwin' dogshit up against *that.*"

Randers nodded slowly. "You right, dude. Somehow we gotta score some mega-buck an' find Cong."

Robby whispered to Donny, "Who's Cong?"

"Vietnamese dude. Sells guns." Donny smiled. "I kinda been wantin' to see him anyways to score some more bullets for the .45. Only he don't come around here much, guess there ain't enough business or somethin'. He's cool. Likes kids. You can tell."

Whitey leaned down. "Yeah. But his stuff *cost.*"

Randers glanced up. "Or what. But his stuff *good.* None of that puss .38 shit."

"Well, maybe he'll give us a trade-up on the .44," said Weasel. "That's a hot gun. Somebody could play Clint E. with it."

"Yeah! An' maybe he give a trade-up on the Army gun, too," said Whitey.

Donny looked sad. "I like that gun a lot," he said to Randers.

Randers nodded. "I hear, dude. But we score a Uzi, you keep it home for us, just like the Army gun."

"Yeah, that be hot. I could keep it Tri-Flowed an' everythin'."

Robby spun a wheel on his board. "Um, you dudes use Tri-Flow 'stead of Speed Cream on your bearin's?"

Kevin pulled out a Camel pack and shook up two cigarettes, holding it out to Robby. "You can use Tri-Flow on your guns too. Saves havin' to score different stuff."

"Oh."

Kevin dug in his pockets and frowned. "Shit! No goddamn matches again! Whitey!"

Whitey fired his Bic. Robby moved closer to Kevin and Kevin leaned down. "I'm sorry if I said somethin' about wipin' your ass, man," said Kevin. "I was just cracked, y'know?"

Robby smiled and shrugged. "It's cool."

Kevin turned to Randers. "So? We gonna score that Bud?"

"Yeah. Then we do some figurin' about this Squeaker thing."

Kevin blew smoke. "Hey, I could get tight with Squeaker. I mean, he's really pretty stupid. Fuck. I could make enough with him in a couple weeks to score us a Uzi. Then we could tell him to fuck-off. *For-ever.*"

Randers frowned. "Duncan say somethin' like that one time. Squeaker so stupid, how come Duncan dead an' not he?"

"Fuck, man! I ain't Duncan. You figure just 'cause I'm white like he was I'm stupid too?"

"Mostly when you talk like that."

"Aw. . . . "

Randers sighed. "Anyway. That only make more probs. Then *we* be sellin' rock to little kids around here. What different us than Squeaker?"

Kevin leaned forward, eyes eager. "No, man! That ain't what I meant. Me an' Weasel could ride up where all the squid-kids hang. They gots all the buck in the world. Shit! Hey, if Weasel took a bath an' wore clean stuff, he'd look just like one of 'em. All them squids hate us anyways; who the fuck cares what happens to 'em?"

Randers spat. "They still kids, ain't they? Hurt just like us. Die just like us—*for*-ever."

"But . . . "

"Butt *out,*" said Donny.

Weasel scratched his head. "Well? Couldn't we just waste Squeaker? I mean, he's got it comin' if anybody does."

Whitey nodded. "Maybe we could pay Eric to put magic on him an' make him die?"

Donny considered. "Um, Nathaniel might kill him for us, if we all asked?"

For just a second Robby thought Randers looked tired. Then Randers sucked a last hit off his cigarette and stomped it out. "Just everybody shut the fuck up. Got no time now for this shit. Maybe whole fuckin' world fallin' apart, but no Squeaker-puss gonna come 'round messin' up our day." He glared at the other boys until they all looked away. "Damn! Squeaker gots all you dudes pissin' in your jeans already an' he not even *done* nuthin' yet. You let dipshit like him ruin you day, you his anyway!" He dropped an arm over Robby's shoulder. "Here a new dude. Not even scared to laugh at T.C. with a Uzi! Maybe he figure we all pusses now."

Randers turned to Robby, touching his lip, the blood smear dried and flaking. "You know me?"

Robby met Randers' eyes a moment, then licked his lip and smiled. "For sure."

"Okay. You comin'?"

"Or what."

Randers snagged his board and the other boys slid off the dumpster. Donny patted Robby's shoulder. "Um, guess I see you around, dude. You can come back to my place tonight, if you wanna."

Robby smiled again. "Thanks, Donny, that'd be cool. Um, so this's *it,* man? I mean, I don't get beat up or have to lick dog-piss or something'?"

Donny smiled back. "You Fresno dudes got a thing for dog-piss? Hey, you can't ride good, everybody know it in two seconds. You're wearin' Randers' blood, what more you want?" He grinned. "I gots another choker at home but you better wait for Randers to think about it."

Robby nodded, lowering his voice. "I hear. But, know what? Way I figure, seems like that Squeaker's gonna be tryin' to kill Randers now."

Kevin came over and put his arm on Robby's shoulder. "Hell. Randers knows that, lame-o."

"Oh."

The other Animals snagged their boards and started to deck. There was a rattle back down the alley and everybody turned as Russel cut around a dumpster. He'd washed his face but his lips were puffy and there was a bruise on one cheek. Kevin scowled and stepped forward. "Let me, man."

"Shut up," said Randers as the boy rolled to him, looking determined and scared. "Wanna do somethin' for me, dude?" Randers asked.

Russel's mouth dropped open and his eyes got big. "For sure, man!"

Randers glanced at Robby. "Got any buck?"

"Fiver." Robby dug out the crumpled sweat-wet bill. Randers took it and looked down at the kid. "You know Cong?"

"For sure, Randers." Russel thought for a minute. "Only, I ain't seen him in awhile...."

Randers handed him the bill. "This yours, dude. You find Cong. Tell him Animals wanna see him. You can't find him, no prob, score the nickel anyway, but you sure the hell better try."

"I find him, Randers! Believe it, man!" Russel jammed the bill in his pocket, then looked up again. "Um, can I have a smoke, man?"

Randers nodded. "Weasel."

Weasel gave the boy a Marlboro and Whitey fired for him.

Russel sucked smoke deep and let it out slow. "Thanks, Randers. Mega! I find Cong, no prob!" He kicked a one-eighty and ripped away.

Randers turned to the others. "Let's book."

Morning sun slanted orange from the east, throwing long shadows. Birds chirped in dry weeds and the air was still cold from night-fog. The smells were morning smells—damp wood and asphalt, wet rusty iron, and chill salt from the Bay. The distant drone of traffic carried from 880.

The Animals and Robby crowded around the van. It was parked under the long roof of an old Navy building, on buckled weedy concrete that was strewn with beer bottles and broken glass. The van faced toward the gates of the huge abandoned storage yard, which sagged half open to the empty waterside street. Its engine idled soft and steady, exhaust ghosting steam into the cool air.

Robby studied the van—new and white and totally factory stock. Maybe it was cleaner; otherwise it looked just like a million others. From inside came faint music, probably a tape, that sounded like ancient Eagles. There was the friendly scent of coffee. Robby liked coffee, and that reminded him of earlier this morning when he'd ridden with the Animals for food at the Center. Kevin drank coffee, too, and had scored him and Robby a cup from the kitchen lady. There'd been all the oatmeal anybody could want, and Robby was hungry enough to eat a big bowlful and ask for more. They'd gotten a sandwich each too. The meat looked and tasted like Spam, but it was warm and good.

He'd seen Nathaniel. The dude didn't look like a werewolf, but then Robby wondered how a real werewolf was supposed to look . . . probably like nothing in the movies. There was something sort of different about him; he moved like a kid for sure. It'd been kind of funny in a way, with so many kids there, that Nathaniel had noticed Robby first thing. Their eyes met for only a second, but it was easy to see that Nathaniel knew Robby was from somewhere else. That other white dude, Alpo, who passed out the food, was okay, but *he* hadn't noticed Robby at all. Randers had talked to Nathaniel for a few minutes in the hall, but the only thing he'd said when they were riding down here later was that Nathaniel was trying to get some old van running so he could take the Animals to someplace called Marineworld. Maybe. At first, Robby thought it was just some kind of mega-mall, but Kevin said he'd seen it on TV and it was totally cool.

Robby checked the Vietnamese dude as he slid out of the van. He looked really young, almost like a kid himself, though Robby always had trouble telling with Viet dudes. Cong was small, even thinner than Rix, and not much taller. His hair was clean and shiny black, cut in a mop like Weasel's, and long but combed. He wore a white T-shirt under a gray canvas jacket, and clean faded jeans over big white Cons. He smelled clean too, not all pussy-perfumed like Squeaker. He had big white teeth, smiled a lot, and his eyes sparkled black and friendly. He talked soft and didn't sound anything like the Vietnamese who ran Quick-Stops.

Cong smiled at the Animals now as he unlocked the van's back doors. Robby pushed forward with the others. The inside looked like some store's gun department, everything in racks or mounted on white plywood.

Weasel poked Whitey. "Check it out, duuude!" Whitey grinned and nodded hard. Rix leaned over both of their shoulders and breathed, "Or what!"

Kevin stood off a little, smoking quietly, though his eyes missed nothing. Donny grinned and nudged Robby. Robby just stared. His head was still a little buzzed from all the beer last night. He didn't remember too much, maybe he'd tried to rap. Oh shit. Now he remembered a lot of giggling and Kevin dragging him to Donny's kid-smelling bed, jerking the blanket over his head and saying, "Dead, *for-ever*," or something like that.

"We wanna check the Uzi," Randers said.

Cong nodded. "For sure, Randers."

Above the sawed-offs were three totally badass-looking guns. All were black and important as hell. One was all metal, stock folded, the same kind T.C. had. The others had more knobs and stuff on them, and one had a small wooden part too. Cong handed Randers the Uzi, unfolding the stock with a kind of Karate chop.

"That's the one everybody wants," Cong said. "Nine-millimeter, select fire, five-fifty rounds per minute on auto, thirty-two round magazine." He knelt beside Randers. "Hold it more like this."

Randers pointed it out toward the Bay.

"Problem for you dudes is small hands," Cong went on. "Check it. See? You have to grip this lever behind the magazine at the same time you pull the trigger or no fire. That's another safety feature so it won't go off by itself if you drop it. A lot of little dudes just tape it down, but I wouldn't carry it on a skateboard that way."

Kevin pointed to another gun. "What's that one, man? Is it better?"

Cong took it down and handed it to Kevin. "Galil. Kind of new. Made by those same badass Jewboys who don't take shit from anybody. Almost a copy of the Russian Kalashnikov without the boilerplate approach. This one's a 7.62, NATO round. A little harder to get ammunition for and about a pound heavier than the Uzi. That could make a difference to you dudes. It's got its own bipod and'll take more thrashing than the Uzi will. Thirty-round magazine."

Kevin checked it carefully. "Yeah? So, is it better than the Uzi?"

Cong considered. "For what you dudes need it for, I'd say not as good. Like, who needs a bipod in the city, and a pound is a pound you know, especially if you're going to be taking it up on a roof."

Kevin nodded.

"Um, what about that other one?" Robby asked.

Cong seemed to study Robby for a moment, then smiled. "Man knows quality!" He handed Robby the gun. "Steyr. German. Nine-millimeter and about a pound lighter than the Uzi. Fires a tad faster too, seven-fifty rounds per minute." He grinned. "And a lot better for small dudes because there's no extra safety to mess with and forget when you're stressed." He took the gun and pulled out the wire stock. "A lot of grown-ups think the stock's too short but it's perfect for you. And, check this. You pull the trigger halfway back and it's semi-auto, all the way back for full. That makes it a lot easier to work in the streets; no switch to flip when you're in a hurry to get something done."

Kevin came over by Robby. "So, it's better than the Uzi?"

Cong nodded. "Totally. Like it was made just for kids. It costs a lot more though."

"Figures," said Weasel.

Robby cradled the gun. It felt good. He pictured T.C. stressed and trying to flip his stupid switch.

"Hey, Donny," Whitey called, pointing. "There's one like yours."

Cong turned. "Oh, yeah. Forty-five, government issue. Nothing high tech, but still about the all-around best for everything." He smiled. "Just a little big to pack on a board a lot."

"You ride, man?" asked Rix.

Cong laughed. "You kidding, dude? Those things are dangerous!"

Weasel giggled. "Too funny!"

Randers held up the Uzi. "How much?"

"But that one's better!" said Kevin, pointing to the Steyr.

"Aw, get real," said Donny. "We probably can't afford even a plain old Uzi."

Cong pulled a pack of Winstons from his jacket pocket, offering them around and firing for the kids with one of those old lighters that still used fluid. "Well, the semi-auto wannabes cost between six and seven bills at the sport shops. I get about a grand for these. They come with the standard thirty-two round magazine, but you should have a couple extra if you're going to be doing much full-auto work."

"Um, you mean, 'wet work,' man? Like in *Soldier of Fortune?*" Donny asked.

Cong grinned. "I never read that shit, dude. It's for wannabes and kids."

"Oh."

"Um," said Rix. "I hear them semi-autos not even sold no more 'cause of some crazy old man shootin' school kids."

Cong sighed. "You mean up in Stockton? Well, that sucked for sure, but this new law is just another typical squid reaction to something that scares 'em. Like a bunch of sheep huddling together and figuring some words on paper will make everything safe again. Hell, Washington D.C. has the toughest gun laws in the country . . . and the most murders. The dudes who shot the Kennedys and King and Lennon didn't need assault rifles, semi or full-auto! Might sound a little gross, but I figure anybody who was flipped out enough to want to kill some kids in a classroom could make just as big a mess with an old six-shooter and a pocketful of extra bullets, or a machete, or a baseball bat. After all, who'd be fighting back?" He considered a minute. "Might not be so easy in one of *your* classrooms though."

Randers handed back the Uzi. Robby expected Cong to wipe it or something, but he didn't. The dude *was* cool.

"So, we need a grand," said Randers.

Cong nodded. "For the Animals, I'll even throw in two extra magazines. Loaded. You dudes are going to be around for awhile. I can tell."

"Maybe," said Randers. He nodded at Donny, who unwrapped the .45 from his shirt while Randers pulled the .44 from the back of his jeans.

Cong gave Donny a smile. "I was wondering what kind of surprise you had there."

"Um, you knew all the time?" asked Whitey.

"Everybody looks, dude. Trouble is, you have to learn to see."

Robby thought of Nathaniel again.

Kevin asked, "Ain't you scared somebody's gonna try an' blow you away sometime?"

Cong grinned and flashed the shoulder holster under his jacket. "Tokarev. Not very high tech either, but it has sentimental value. Belonged to my dad. He used to tell me this country lost the war because it couldn't see the bad guys from the good anymore. Like, everybody looks at what you kids have to live in, but nobody wants to *see* it. Seems, when you see something you don't like, you have to deal

100

with it somehow on a personal level, and that might be scary or uncomfortable. A lot easier to put words on paper and make believe the cops and politicians will keep everything under control." He grinned again. "Sheep payin' wolves to protect 'em. Trouble is, someday there might not be enough to go around and those wolves are going to be the only things left with teeth." He laughed. "Somehow I think you dudes will get by." He sighed again and shrugged. "Oh well."

Cong turned back to Randers. "That's the only way for you small dudes to carry big guns, like you were just now, back of your jeans with the barrel poking your butt. Keep your shirt tied around your waist and hanging down like that, only not so tight. I know it's uncomfortable as hell and it won't get by any cop who's worth a shit, and you'd better hope you never wipe out on your board, but little dudes like you don't have many choices."

"Or what!" said Donny.

Cong smiled at him and shrugged once more. " 'Fraid it's the same everywhere for kids, man—San Francisco, Portland, L.A., Seattle . . . "

"Fresno," said Robby.

Rix poked Weasel. "Um, what war was he talkin', man?"

"I don't know, Iran or somethin'."

"You give trade-ups?" asked Randers.

Cong glanced at the big .44. "I remember that one. Little white dude bought it a few months back."

"He give it to me," said Randers.

Cong nodded. "I remember. He wanted a big one for you. Dude thought a lot of you, man. Wanted a .357, but I didn't have any more right then. Really, I tried to talk him out of this one. What kid wants a .44 anymore besides some white skinhead junior KKK wannabe, but he said he couldn't wait. That's a hard gun to move." He winked at Robby. "Except in Fresno. I sold it cheap."

Cong took the .45 from Donny. He pulled the clip, worked the action a few times, then stuck a corner of his T-shirt in the chamber and looked down the barrel. "Mmmm. Not one of mine but in pretty good shape." He smiled at Donny. "You keep it clean, dude. That's cool. Don't use it much though, do you?"

"Naw. Bullets cost."

Cong turned back to Randers and thought a minute. "Sounds like you've got a problem you're trying to solve, dude?"

"Yeah."

"Takes fire to fight fire, don't it?"

"Yeah."

Cong studied the boys for awhile. "Well, the .44's no problem, but I can't give you much on it. See, I'll just have to take it to one of those wannabe gun shows." He grinned. "Sell it to some closet Nazi or nervous Silicon with a dick the size of a Beanie-Weenie who thinks bigger is better."

The kids snickered.

"Anyway," Cong went on, "I'd hate to see a street kid try and get ammo for that dinosaur in a hurry." He looked at Randers. "I really did try to talk your friend out of it."

Randers nodded. "I hear. He dead now anyways."

"Fire?"

"Naw," said Kevin. "Dipshit jumped off a buildin'. Did it to himself."

Cong still looked at Randers. "I'm sorry, man." He studied the .45 again. "This is worth more, but the numbers are filed. Sloppy. A lot of people don't like that." He smiled again. "Some little badass showtime with a voice that sounds like it's never going to get through the change was bitching to me awhile back that he had his .45 rousted right out of his car." Cong glanced at Donny. "Were the numbers already filed, man?"

Donny nodded.

Cong worked the action again. "Well, I could have my cousin touch up this butcher job and re-blue it—a lot of work and it can still be X-rayed. But it's a pretty good piece." He turned back to Randers. "I can give you three in trade on both, dude. Best I can do. Really."

Rix sighed. "Shit. Seven bills."

"Suckorama," said Weasel.

Randers scuffed his big Cheetahs in broken glass and thought.

"Hey, man," said Kevin. "I can do it! The way I told you! Gimme two weeks."

Cong glanced around at the quiet boys. "Anybody want a Coke?" Everybody nodded.

Cong went around to the front of his van, then returned, shaking ice from a sixer. He handed them out. Tabs popped in the morning stillness. "Sorry, no beer."

Randers finally shrugged. "It cool. Thanks, man." He glanced at Kevin and frowned. "No! Not that way," then looked up at Cong. "Figure we just take some more bullets for what we gots now."

"An' another clip-thing for my .45," added Donny.

Kevin spat. "Fuck! This's dogshit, man!"

Cong gave Kevin a long considering look, then took back the Galil, slipping it into its rack. Robby was still fingering the Steyr. Cong gave him another wink then turned to Randers. "For sure. Um, you have a second, man?"

Randers followed Cong around to the front of the van. "They won't roust nuthin'," he said.

Cong smiled. "I know. Shitfire, man, if I didn't think you and your dudes were cool, you figure I'd let you get close to me with two loaded guns? Let 'em look." He studied Randers. "I figure you know what is as much as anybody, man, probably a lot more than most no matter how old they are. But, I think maybe that Kevin is going to disappoint you someday."

Randers shrugged. "Squeaker workin' on him, same he done Duncan."

Cong thought awhile longer then nodded to himself. He reached in the van and pulled out a little gun. It looked a lot like a .45, only smaller. "Stick this in your jeans. Now! And don't ever tell anybody you have it. *Anybody.* It's a .380 Bersa, Argentine. Not a bad little piece, took it on a trade. It's loaded. Small enough to fire from a skateboard if you have to. Here's another magazine. You can figure it out later, alone." He smiled. "You owe me one sometime, dude."

Randers frowned slightly. "Why you do this, man?"

"Ever hear the story about the rat and the Lion?"

"Uh uh."

"Forget it. Kid-story anyway. For sure I hate to think about you dudes going up against an Uzi with what you have now."

103

"You *know?*"

"I *see,* remember? Listen! An Uzi looks bad as hell, makes a lot of noise and spits a lot of bullets. Trouble is, most dudes can't hit anything over fifty feet away except by accident. Hell, throw enough lead out there and you have to hit something eventually. Most of the kids dig that full-auto too much, never practice aiming at anything with the semi. T.C.'s pretty small. I can't see where he's even got the muscle to hold the muzzle down. He drinks a lot of Heinie, and I can't see where he does anything but sit on his ass in that car and look bad. Be lucky to run a block and has all the moves of a jellyfish in a bucket of baby oil." Cong shrugged. "Best I can do, dude."

Randers sighed and nodded, slipping the little gun in the front of his jeans and yanking down his T-shirt. "Thanks. Um, why you do this? *Really?*"

"I always figured there's three types of people in this world, man—good, bad, and evil. What you call the squids decide for you about the good and bad, those are just words, like hot and cold. And they change all the time. I mean, it's totally okay to shoot kids in a 'war'—then you're 'good.' A cop is always 'good,' even if he's beating the shit out of some eight-year-old in an alley. Everybody does 'good' things; once in awhile you might have to do a 'bad' thing to stay good. Maybe you can't hear me, but sometimes I figure if Jesus had an Uzi instead of a whip, he'd have used it. Anyway, evil is always evil. A dude has to decide to be evil, and he *knows* what it is." Cong sighed. "I have to deal with everybody, man, but I don't always like it. This's a pretty good country, if half the assholes weren't asleep or too lazy to do their part running it. Only, there's a war going on and you kids are fighting it and the squids are hoping that both sides lose."

Randers nodded again. "I hear, man. Enough."

Cong put his hand on Randers' shoulder. "Carry lots of Band-Aids, dude."

Robby put a Milky Way on the counter and smiled at the fat white lady.

She glanced up from her paper. "Fifty cents."

Robby dug in his pocket, the lining stretched tight because of the .45

stuck in the back of his jeans and covered by his shirt. He put up two quarters. "Um, could I get some matches, please?"

The fat lady scooped up the money. "We don't give matches to kids."

Robby squirmed a little. The heavy gun hurt his ass and the front sight cut him. "Um, maybe I could buy some?"

The fat lady frowned. "We don't sell matches to kids. Now, go on!"

Robby carried his board to the door. "Bitch," he whispered.

Kevin was sitting on the curb out front, spinning his wheels. "Score some?"

"Naw. Hosebag wouldn't give me any!" Robby unwrapped the candy bar, broke it in two, and gave half to Kevin. "Wanna try, man? Maybe she'll give you some 'cause you're white!"

Kevin jammed it all in his mouth at once and talked around it. "Get real, dude." He slapped his sweaty chest. "Only thing bein' white gets you is the dirt shows more." He snatched up the Marlboro pack lying beside him and shoved it in his pocket. "Fuck! I wanted a smoke, man. Too bad you went an' lost your fuckin' lighter."

Robby shrugged. "I always lose things. My dad used to yell at me a lot 'cause of that." He sat beside Kevin, board between his knees, and they both stared at the ground. Robby kept shifting because the gun poked him. "Anyway, I wanted a smoke too. Sure wish Squeaker would come around an' get dead so's I can stop carryin' this fuckin' thing. Like, it was cool at first, but it sucks now. Wanna carry it awhile?"

Kevin snickered, wiping chocolate off his chin. "No way! Randers said for you to carry it an' he seems kinda pissed at me lately anyhow. 'Sides, it's a pain in the ass."

Robby giggled. "Too funny, dude." Inside, the fat lady looked up and scowled.

Kevin glanced at the Marlboro pack half sticking out of his pocket. "I seen in this movie once where this dude lights a cigarette just by shootin' it. Figure that really works? We could light one that way an' another one off it."

Robby considered that. "I don't know. Only, wouldn't Randers get pissed 'cause we wasted a whole bullet?"

"Yeah. The way he's been all hyper, it's better not to fuck around."

"Well, Jeez. Wouldn't *you* be hyper if somebody wanted to kill you?"

"Yeah. I guess."

The fat lady came to the door. "You kids go on now! You can't play here! And, don't ride those things on the sidewalk."

Robby sighed and stood, making sure the gun was still covered. They decked and rolled across the Quick-Stop parking lot while the fat lady watched.

"Like to ride 'em up her fuckin' wazoo till she sings," Kevin muttered.

"Douchebag," Robby added.

They cut around the gas pumps. It was hot again and there was nothing to do. In a way, Robby thought, Oakland wasn't much different from Fresno. "Um, how come we're up here in squid city anyhow?" he asked. "For sure you don't figure Squeaker hangs here?"

Kevin shrugged. "Naw. Sometimes I just like to get outa dogshit-land for a little while. Watch the real people. We can go back if you wanna."

The light changed on the corner, and they rolled across the street. All the crossing curbs were sloped like ramps. They cut around and slapped the regular curb. The buildings were all low and far apart with grass strips and trees in between.

"Kinda looks like Blackstone Avenue in Fresno," Robby said.

"Yeah? You, um, miss Fresno, man? I thought you told me you was happy here."

They rolled down clean sidewalk. Kevin tailed and sat on a grass berm under the dappled shade of a tree. Robby sat beside. The grass smelled good above the exhaust stink.

"Naw," said Robby. "Only, sometimes I miss the dudes, Jeffers an' Tad an' Jamie an' Ryan. Jamie an' Ryan are white, but like you said, who cares. Jeffers would like you too. He was kinda my best friend. Sorta like Randers in a way. He always knew what to do, y'know?"

Kevin lay back in the soft grass, head pillowed on his arms. Robby couldn't because of the gun.

"Yeah," said Kevin. He looked up at Robby. "You, um, see a lot of stuff, man. You figure, if anything ever happened to Randers, the dudes would want me talkin for 'em?"

Robby thought awhile. "Probably, I guess. I mean, you always seem to know what to do too—when you ain't cracked-out."

Kevin waved a hand. "Aw, I only do that when I'm bored."

Robby nodded. "Well, next to Randers, you kick ass an' ride the best." Robby pulled up his legs and rested his chin on his knees. "It's kinda funny, the way a lot of dudes are the same, y'know? I mean, Weasel an' Whitey are almost like Jamie an' Ryan. Rix too. I mean, they're good dudes an' can fight an' ride an' everythin', but it's like they need a Randers to keep 'em alive."

Kevin nodded, reaching over and tugging Robby's shirt back to hide the gun butt. "Yeah. I hear. What about that other dude, Tad?"

Robby smiled. "He's like Russel, almost. Only older. Sometimes we wonder how he keeps alive at all." Robby was quiet a moment. Finally, he looked down at Kevin. "Um, maybe you shouldn't even be askin' me stuff like that. I mean, I only been here four days, an' I don't even know all the words yet."

"Maybe. But you still know a lot of stuff, an' you're kinda different."

Robby smiled again. "Bad different or good different?"

"Different where I gotta think to talk to ya. So? Where you sleepin' tonight?"

"Maybe at Donny's again."

"Heard you stayed with Randers last night."

"Yeah. Only, he don't sleep too good. Kicks an' talks a lot."

"I know. Whenever I stay with Nathaniel, he does the same thing. Then sometimes he just leaves in the middle of the night an' don't come back till the sun's up again." Kevin looked at Robby. "Um, it gets sorta scary alone in that big old buildin' at night. Them radiator things make all kind of weird sounds." Kevin looked away. "Sometimes I pull the fuckin' blanket over my head. Sounds puss, huh?"

"No it don't, man. I done that. Lots of times!"

"Yeah?"

"For sure." Robby thought a minute. "Um, you figure Nathaniel goes out 'cause he's a werewolf?"

Kevin shrugged. "Maybe. All I know is I'd rather see him grow fur an' claws right there beside me than stay alone in that old spook-house all night. One time I woke up so hungry it hurt an' I kept thinkin' of that huge fridge in the kitchen, but no way was I leavin' Nathaniel's room!"

Robby smiled. "Well, what if you gotta . . . "

"I'd do it out the fuckin' window! Um, would you wanna sleep there, too, with me sometime?"

Robby giggled. "Nathaniel must got a huge bed."

Kevin snickered. "Naw. I sleep on the floor unless I get super lonely. Um, you'd have to, too, but there's lots of blankets."

"For sure. That's be hot. Tonight."

"For sure! Um, you know any good dirty jokes?"

"Well, there's this one about a lady who buys a dog named Free-show. Wanna hear it?"

"Not now, man. Wait till tonight. Maybe Nathaniel ain't heard it neither."

Robby nodded and squirmed again. "Jeez! I'm really starting to hate this fuckin' gun, man! Seems like Squeaker can make you hurt even when he ain't around. Um, do you know him very good?"

Kevin stared up at the tree branches and the sky. "Aw, not too good. He used to be just another dude who sat by me in class. He always was kinda puss. You figure he sounds funny now, you shoulda heard him when he was little. But he was still okay sometimes. Even rode a board for a while, only never got very good." Kevin was quiet a few minutes, thinking. "Me an' Rix got totally drunk with him one time, fifth grade I think. He was pretty funny, knew a lot of hot jokes. Too bad we gotta kill him."

"Yeah. It makes it hard when you can see somethin' even a little good in somebody, man. Like, you wish you could make the good part come, y'know?"

"Yeah. Only nobody gots time to make the good part come."

There was a soft chittering overhead and Robby looked up. Two squirrels sat on a branch. Robby smiled and poked Kevin in the ribs, pointing. "Check it, man. Kinda cute ain't they, like little baby things."

Kevin snickered. "Yeah? Figures they'd have things like them up here in squid-land. Probably put 'em there for decorations or some-

thin'. Fuck, when you gots money, everythin's cute!" He grinned.
"Watch it, dude! They'll probably shit on us! Anyway, take away their
cute little tails an' what you got? Rats in the trees."

There were rattles, wheels clicking cracks, and three white boys
came ripping up the sidewalk. Robby and Kevin checked boards, new
ones; a Hammerhead, Fred Smith, and a Zorlac. They were pretty hard
ridden, even if the kids were totally clean.

"Yo, dude," Kevin called to the biggest who looked about his age.
He was chubbier than Robby, that soft floppy kind. Robby figured
another year and the dude wouldn't be riding anymore. He was blond
and tan, shirt around his waist like the others.

All the boys tailed, looking down at Robby and Kevin. "Yeah,
dude?" the chubby one asked.

Kevin sat up. "Got any matches?"

The three boys looked at each other a minute. "Maybe," said the
chubby one. "Got any smokes?"

Kevin smiled and held up his pack.

"All right!" said the littlest, who looked about ten.

Everybody took cigarettes and the chubby boy pulled a little box
from his pocket. Robby checked it. The box was made of wood and
had a cartoon of a man in a rowboat. The matches were wooden too,
but smaller than the ones Robby's mom used to light her stove. The
chubby kid fired and all leaned together for the flame. Robby sat back
and breathed smoke. The first cigarette in a long time was always the
best. "Them's hot matches, dude."

The chubby boy handed him the box. "Or what! Check 'em out!
They're even waterproof."

"Well," said the middle boy. "They don't light underwater or
nuthin'. We tried it once. But if you drop 'em in the toilet or somethin'
they'll still work."

"If you wanna touch 'em after," added the littlest.

"Yeah?" said Robby. "So, where can you score 'em, man?"

The chubby boy pointed across the parking lot. "K-Mart sometimes.
The cash register people don't always pay attention to what a kid
buys."

"Only, that don't work with beer," said the middle boy.

"Or smokes," said the littlest. "Too bad, huh?"

"All right," said Robby, handing back the box. He turned to Kevin. "Maybe we'll check that out sometime."

The chubby boy gave Robby the box again. "Aw, keep 'em, brother. I got another one. I can see you're all poor an' everything."

The littlest looked around and then knelt in front of Robby. "Um, you got any crack, brother?"

Robby frowned. "No."

The middle boy poked the little one. "Told ya, dippo!" He shrugged at Robby. "Sorry, brother. He asks that every time he sees a black dude. I told him he's gonna get the shit kicked outa him someday."

The chubby boy rolled his board back and forth and grinned at Kevin. "Hey. How many flies does it take to screw in a light bulb?"

Kevin glanced at Robby and they both shrugged.

"Two. But I don't know how the hell they got in there!"

The squid-kids snickered while Robby and Kevin grinned. "Too funny, man," said Robby.

"Well." The chubby boy decked. "Thanks for the smokes. Later, dudes."

Robby nodded. "Or what. Thanks for the fire."

The three boys rolled.

Kevin stood. "Guess we better start back, *brother.*"

Robby snickered. "Yeah? Well, 'case you ain't noticed, man, you're a nigger too. Just a white one."

Kevin laughed. It was the first time Robby'd heard him laugh. "Hell, I figured that out a long time ago."

"There's too much fire!"

Whitey threw a bottle at Rix. Rix, poking at the little fire on the concrete floor, dodged easily, and the other Animals laughed as the bottle flew past and shattered somewhere in the shadows. Rix knocked away part of the fire with a piece of pipe and stomped it out. "Hard to control fire, man," he muttered. "Always wants to go nuke when nobody's lookin'."

Randers took a hit of Bud and studied the hot dog sizzling on the end of the stick he held. Around the fire the other kids did the same, except Kevin, who sat cross-legged and quiet, smoking and staring into the flames. There were four empty bottles beside him and another half empty between his legs.

"Um, you gonna be wasted to the max, man," Donny told him.

Kevin shrugged, not looking up. "Who gives a shit?"

Robby, next to him, glanced at Kevin's face in the flickering light. It looked more tired than anything else. Kevin hadn't talked much at the Center last night; Nathaniel hadn't been there at all. They'd slept together in Nathaniel's bed, and Robby had kept waking up to the creepy shiftings and creakings of the old building, the scent of Nathaniel in his nostrils, a strong male smell that was somehow wild, bringing a tightness to his throat and a stirring in his loins and a strange yearning that couldn't be explained. A werewolf would probably smell like that. They'd left early, before Leese and Alpo came in, skating down along the foggy water until Kevin, looking restless, said he had to go home for a little while and rolled away alone. Robby'd spent most of the day at Donny's watching TV.

Robby touched Kevin's arm, but Kevin didn't seem to notice. Randers took a bite of hot dog and looked up at Rix. "Just keep it down, man. Somebody outside here might see."

The third floor of the old warehouse was huge and empty. The kids' voices awakened echoes, though they spoke low and quietly. Blackness surrounded the small circle of firelight, and the ruddy glow lit faces and glittered in eyes. Fog wafted thick and cold through broken windows, hanging with the smoke against the high roof. The talk and whispers faded a moment though the soft echoes seemed to go on by themselves in the dark distant corners. Weasel leaned forward, amber eyes glinting bright. "Wanna hear a ghost story?"

Randers looked across at him and nodded, and the others all turned toward Weasel.

"Well, there's this dude named Mark, an' he was skatin' home one night, only it's totally late an' he figures he can take a shortcut through this graveyard. . . . "

All the boys got quiet, the soft crackle of fire the only sound.

"So. There he is, right? In the middle of this huge dark graveyard, all alone."

111

Whitey squirmed a little. "Um, how old was he, man?"

Kevin frowned. "Same's us, dipshit."

"Hey, have you heard this before?" demanded Weasel.

"Uh uh."

"Well, then how do you know?"

"Um," said Robby. "Maybe 'cause you always figure them dudes in stories are just like you?"

"Oh," said Weasel. "Yeah, right."

"So? Was he black?" asked Rix.

"Tell it, Weasel," said Randers. "Everybody else shut up."

"Anyways. The dude's all alone in this dark scary graveyard. 'Course he's gotta carry his board 'cause it's all grass between the tombstones. He's just about to the middle when he hears this voice start callin', 'Mark, Mark, Mark . . .' "

"Fuck!" whispered Rix.

"So, he starts runnin', y'know? Tryin' to get to the other side. Now the voice is behind him, 'Mark, Mark, Mark!' An' it's gettin' closer too. So, I mean this dude gets hyper. Starts bookin' warp-speed or what! An' all the time 'cross this lonely graveyard the voice keeps comin' closer an' closer, 'Mark, Mark, Mark!' "

Robby set down his beer and leaned closer to the fire, feeling Kevin's shoulder against his own.

"So then," Weasel went on, "he gets to where he can see the graveyard gates on the other side, only they're still so far, far away. I mean, this dude puts it in warp seven! But then, he trips over this tombstone an' eats shit!"

"Oh, Jeez!" said Whitey, pushing against Rix.

"An' here's that voice comin' on fast, 'Mark, Mark, Mark!' So, like the dude figures he's total history, right? He looks up, an' outa the dark comes this . . ."

"What?" breathed Donny, mouth open.

"This harelip *dog!*"

"Shit!" bawled Whitey.

Rix flipped Weasel the finger. "Fuck you, man! That ain't no ghost story."

"Just a fuckin' dumb old joke," said Donny.

112

Randers smiled a little and sipped beer.

"Hey," said Rix. "I just remembered one, an' it a real ghost story, too. See, there's this dude with a golden arm . . . *real* gold. . . . "

Kevin sighed and chugged beer. Robby gave him a slight shrug and a smile and took a swallow of his own Bud, looking around at the darkness, not really listening to Rix. Smells of hot dogs and boys, of beer and cigarettes and fire, were in his nose. He got up, automatically snagging his board, and walked across to a window. Only Kevin and Randers seemed to notice. Robby leaned his board against the wall and stood, sipping beer and gazing out at the fog.

There was a shadow beside him and a shoulder brushed his own. He didn't have to look; all dudes smelled different. Kevin held out his Marlboros and Robby took one, firing with the squid-kid's waterproof matches.

The two boys stared out at the fog.

Kevin sighed smoke. "Can't figure what Randers so paranoid about. We been makin' fires here ever since we was all little. Nobody never notices. Anyway, the fog's so fuckin' thick tonight you can't even see the street."

"Yeah," said Robby. "It gets like this in Fresno too."

"Yeah? Um, don't you need a ocean or somethin' to make fog?"

"I don't know. It just comes. Get's all dark an' scary like this an' you can't even hear nuthin' a block away. Makes it real easy to just go ridin' off a curb into a truck or somethin'."

Kevin nodded. The fog was chill and he moved closer to Robby. "Yeah. Just like here." He took a swallow of Bud. "Um, what's Fresno really like, man? Is it any better than here at all? In any way?"

Robby felt that he should tell Kevin it was better. But, why? "Naw," he said finally. "It sucks for kids . . . just like everyplace else. 'Least, for kids like us." He killed the beer, still feeling like he should've said something else. "I'm sorry, man," he added.

Kevin smiled. Robby couldn't see his face, but he felt a smile in the dark. Kevin put his arm over Robby's shoulders, his smokey breath warm on Robby's cheek. "Y'know," said Kevin, "you say 'I'm sorry' more 'n anybody I ever seen. If I didn't know you better I might think you was a puss or somethin'. Hey, everythin' that's dogshit ain't your fault, y'know? I mean, what'er you sorry for?"

Robby shrugged. "I can't make the words come. Sometimes I just get the feelin' stuff ain't what it's really supposed to be like. I mean, I come all that way, maybe a thousand miles even, an' it's just the same. I wonder if squid-kids are happy, man?"

"Well, even them three yesterday didn't have no smokes. . . . "

Behind, Rix's voice suddenly bawled, "*You* got it!" Donny gave a yell and the other boys laughed.

"I remember that one now," said Robby.

Kevin nodded. "I do too. Sometimes I figure I heard everythin' all before."

There was a noise in the stairwell. The other kids scattered into the shadow. Kevin grabbed Robby's arm. "Freeze!" he hissed. "Nobody can see if us we stay still."

Robby watched the empty firelit circle from the corner of his eye. Russel came slowly into the glow, carrying his board and looking around like he expected ghosts to fly at him any second. The Animals returned out of darkness and surrounded the little boy, but he ignored all except Randers.

"What's up, dude?" Randers asked.

Russel moved close to him. "Squeaker say he need to see you, man. Say, in a hour at the Navy yard. Say, he gots mega-buck an' need Animal shredders to do a thing. Say, be sure an' tell you it no rock deal. No kids gonna get fucked."

Weasel snickered. "Oh, yeah. Ain't nuthin' Squeaker ever do don't gots rock in it somewheres."

"An' don't end up fuckin' kids too," added Whitey.

"Shut up," said Randers. "Story an' joke time over." He turned as Robby and Kevin came back from the window. "Robby, you be carryin' that gun for days now. Donny show you how to work it?"

"Yeah. Only, I never shot it."

"You ever shoot a gun?"

"Jeffers' old .38, once."

"This kick more," Donny said. "You gotta be ready for that."

Randers glanced at Whitey. "Give Kevin the .44. He carry it tonight."

Whitey pulled the big gun from his jeans, then studied Kevin. "Shit, man! He totally wasted! Check him out!"

"Yeah," said Rix. "Dude can't even walk right."

Randers scowled, the angles of his face hard in the fireglow. "Don't fuck with me! Give him the gun."

Kevin took it, stuck it in the back of his jeans, then turned to Randers. "So? What's the plan?"

Randers spat on the floor. "Plan? Get real! Go close by Squeaker an' kill him! That the only plan we got. T.C. worth a shit for a bodyguard, he try an' not let you. Simple."

Randers looked at Robby. "Can you kill?"

Robby felt a tightness in his throat. "What can I say, man? I just seen three dudes get shot on TV today. It can't be *that* hard. Um, but if I start goin' puss or somethin', maybe I can give the gun to somebody else?"

Randers nodded. "Yeah. You good dude, runaway-Robby. 'Case you accidentally go puss, give it over to Weasel."

"Um," asked Rix. "Do we gotta kill Calvin too? I mean, he used to be a pretty good dude."

Randers suddenly had a handful of Rix's T-shirt, yanking the taller boy's face close to his own, his voice husky and strained. "Hear me! All you! Calvin not Calvin no more. He T.C. with a Uzi! He *kill* you! Dead *for*-ever. Like Duncan be now! Graveyard! Worm food, god-dammit!" Randers let go of Rix and looked around. "Now. Got to figure maybe Squeaker gots a Uzi, too, all his buck. Squeaker want me only, but he kill you all he think he need to. Hear?"

"Shit," said Weasel. "Even if he kills you, man, we'd never do nuthin' for that cocksucker!"

Randers smiled a little and gripped Weasel's shoulder. "I know, dude." Then he glanced at Kevin. "But Squeaker 'sposed to be stupid, remember? Maybe figure, me dead, next dude be talkin' for Animals listen to he."

"Um," asked Whitey. "Who *would* you want talkin' for us, 'case you did get killed?"

"Kevin."

The other boys exchanged glances, then nods. Kevin studied Randers a moment then looked at the floor. Robby moved close and touched Kevin's arm.

Randers turned back to the others. "Okay. We ride over the back way. Climb the fence. Squeaker gonna cruise his puss-car right in the front gates, believe it, 'cause that the way they do on TV an' he be total showtime. Prob'ly stop where Cong be the other day. We get there, maybe we got time for more figurin'." He glanced at Kevin again. "Make a plan. You ride all right, man?"

Kevin met Randers' eyes. "Or what."

Randers nodded. "You a good dude too. Whatever happen." He swung around. "Donny! You go home."

"Aw..."

Randers took Donny's shoulders. "Hear me, dude. This 'portant. You gots the doctor stuff I score from my mom, remember? Animals need what you do good. Maybe this over 'fore you mom get home, we come there. Other way, anybody hurt, maybe we make it to the Center. Nathaniel help."

Donny finally nodded. "Yeah. Okay. If I don't see anybody by the time she come home, I'll sneak out an' meet you at the Center. They already gots a big first-aid box there."

"Yeah. You smart like I always know. Only, don't say nuthin' to Nathaniel till we all together again. Cops can't figure him. Don't like him. Better he not know nuthin' 'bout this till it done." Randers knelt and gave Russel a quick hug. "You good dude too, Russel-man. You do somethin' for me?"

"For sure! I could shoot a gun!"

Randers smiled. "Uh uh. You time maybe come sooner than you want. You mom be pissed, you not home tonight?"

"Aw, she always pissed over somethin', man. No prob."

"Okay. You go with Donny. Help with the doctor stuff. Maybe run message."

Russel looked disappointed, but nodded. "For sure, Randers."

Randers stood again and gazed around at the other boys. "Okay. Let's book!"

The Animals snagged their boards and headed for the stairs. Donny caught Robby's arm as he passed. "Don't forget the safety, man. Just leave it off after you cock it."

"Right," said Robby, watching the other boys disappear down the black stairwell. "Um, one thing I can't figure. How come Randers ain't carryin' the .44? I mean, it's *him* Squeaker really wants dead."

Donny glanced toward the stairs, frowning in the dying fireglow. "Yeah. I don't know, man. Somethin' weird happenin' for sure." He faced Robby and gripped his arm. "But, listen. Randers know what is. You gonna be a Animal, you got to always hang on to that or you're dead meat. Randers say, 'Skate in front of that truck,' well, you just gotta trust him, that's all. It'd be the same with Mason if you was a Rat. For sure Randers take any one of us anytime, but that ain't the reason the dudes listen to him; it 'cause he the smartest. Bullets don't give a shit how bad a kid is. I know Randers since first grade, man. Duncan's the only dude he ever lost an' that only 'cause Duncan stop listenin' to him." Donny smiled. "An' that why *you* carryin' the Army gun now, 'cause Randers know you. For sure Weasel an' Whitey okay, but maybe they forget about the safety or somethin'. Rix? Well, he die for you, but he probably only drop a gun an' shoot his ownself. See, all Animals good dudes, but they good in they own special ways." He grinned. "Like me. Um, you scared, Robby?"

"Kinda. A little."

"Mmmm. Well, remember, Squeaker kill you, man. Not TV dead. *Dead,* dead! *For*-ever!"

Robby nodded slowly. "Yeah. Well, like I said before, I don't see you again, thanks."

Donny slapped Robby's shoulder. "Aw, you see me again, dude. Believe it. Be up at my place drunk on your ass tomorrow. Read all my comics. That my man."

"Um?"

"Yeah?"

"If I did die tonight, would you keep my board? By your bed like Duncan's?"

"Mmmm, for sure. Only, don't you figure Kevin might want it? I mean, he needs a new board to the max."

117

Robby thought a moment. "Yeah. You're right. I'd like for Kevin to be ridin' it."

Donny gave Robby a hug and Robby hugged the fat kid back. "Now, book," said Donny. "Thundercats, ho!"

"If a Uzi shoot fifty-five bullets a minute, an' T.C. gots a thirty-two bullet clip, how long 'fore he got no more bullets?"

Weasel gave Randers a shrug. "Fuck, I don't know, man. I ain't no good in school." He grinned. "But I can tell you why six is scared of seven."

Whitey turned. " 'Cause seven ate nine, dipshit. That's so *old*."

"Aw, school sucks," said Rix.

"Shut up!" hissed Randers. "Shit! Sound like a bunch of goddamn kids here." He looked at Robby. "You figure it out, man?"

"Maybe, if I had some paper. But, for sure T.C.'s gonna be out of bullets really fast on full-auto."

"Yeah?" Kevin muttered. "Wonder how long it takes to put in a new clip, or how many of 'em he gots? That's the kinda stuff we should know."

The boys pressed together in the cold darkness of the empty building. Robby could smell their tenseness, but no fear. He suddenly wished Nathaniel's scent was with them too. Rix stood by the big sliding door, watching through a crack. Outside, under the long roof, fog swirled thick in night breeze. Rix jammed his face closer to the crack. "Lights comin' through the gate!"

Randers looked around at the Animals. It was too dark to see faces but he touched them one by one. "Okay, do like we figured. You all good dudes. Book!"

Whitey, Weasel, and Rix ran back toward a line of windows showing as pale squares in the blackness. They carried their boards. Kevin and Robby stayed by the door with Randers. Randers touched Robby again. "You don't gotta be here, dude."

"Ain't I a Animal now?"

Randers' teeth showed for a second. "For sure. Score you a choker tomorrow."

The glow of headlights lit the fog and tires crunched gravel as the black 'Vette cruised up slow onto weedy concrete and stopped, engine idling deep and fierce. "Deja vu," murmured Kevin.

Robby put his hand on Randers' hard-muscled arm. "That cement's kinda thrashed out there, man. It ain't gonna be easy to skate in the dark."

"I put on some old Kryptonic 70s today. They handle that shit."

"Maybe," said Kevin. "Keep out of the headlights, dude."

Randers studied Kevin's face in the dim glow filtering through the door cracks. "Yeah. I remember that, man."

Kevin already had the .44 out in his hand. Robby pulled the .45 from his jeans, cocking it the way Donny had showed him, safety off, hammer back. Donny said it would kick up, shoot high. Robby wondered what they would feel like.

Randers shoved open the door, decked, and rolled, cutting wide around the back of the 'Vette, his form glowing blood red for a moment in the tail lights. Robby and Kevin crouched together in the doorway and waited.

"Maybe all Squeaker wants is just to talk," Robby whispered.

Kevin spat. "Yeah, right."

The 'Vette's passenger door opened, and T.C. slid out fast, looking all around. He shifted his Uzi, finger on the trigger, staring hard a moment toward the dark doorway, then turned to watch Randers. He wasn't wearing a shirt and the big gold chain glittered against his chubby chest as the car's headlights reflected from the fog. Robby wondered if T.C. thought he looked badder that way. Really, he looked like a little boy playing Rambo. Robby couldn't see his face too well, but the kid's movements were uncertain.

The other door opened and Squeaker got out, smooth and wary, watching as Randers cut way over to the edge of the concrete slab. Robby noticed that Squeaker kept one hand inside on the dash. Squeaker's teeth glinted as he grinned. "Hey! Rander-man! You skate too fuckin' much. Come here an' talk like real men do."

Randers cut a slow eight, still out on the edge. Robby could hear gravel spit from under the big Kryptonics and the occasional crunch of glass. He knew the concrete was buckled and full of big cracks. "Jeez," he whispered. "It's hard enough to skate that shit in daytime."

Kevin said nothing, but shifted his position so that he was crouching almost behind Robby.

"Naw," called Randers. "I just a skate-punk nigger-boy, remember? I never get to be real important man like you!"

T.C. kept looking around, alert, but Robby wondered if he and Squeaker were really stupid enough to think Randers would come alone, or that the other Animals would let him. "They act like they don't know about our guns, man," whispered Robby.

Kevin's voice came out of the darkness. "I told Randers Squeaker was stupid."

Robby squatted, holding the gun out with both hands, trying to keep T.C.'s chest in the sights. The .45 was heavy as hell. He knew the .44 weighed even more, and was about to turn to see how Kevin held it. Then, from the fog, carrying above the 'Vette's steady idle, came the sound of skateboard wheels on rough concrete.

"It's startin'," Robby whispered. Suddenly, he felt something cold against his neck.

"Just stay still, dude!" Kevin hissed.

The skate sounds got louder. T.C.'s head jerked up and he stared around. Squeaker seemed to hear the rattles too, and his wary glances reminded Robby of the squirrels in the trees. Then, a beer bottle arced out of the fog and smashed on the 'Vette's windshield. Squeaker grabbed for something on the dash as glass pieces sprayed around him. T.C. fired blindly into the night, flame spitting orange from the Uzi's muzzle.

More bottles followed from three directions, some missing the car and shattering across pavement. Robby saw Squeaker snag another Uzi off the dash. Suddenly hate flooded Robby and he forgot Kevin, swinging the .45's sights over on Squeaker. Then, something exploded in his ear.

"Shit!" yelled Robby, as hot gunpowder air seared his cheek.

Kevin's voice sounded faint in Robby's numbed ears, even though he was probably yelling above the Uzi's stuttering blast. "Sorry! I was tryin' to steady the fuckin' gun on your shoulder!"

Robby jerked the .45's trigger, aiming at the Uzi's flame, feeling the big gun buck in his hands. "Don't. You hurt my ears, goddammit!"

Behind him, Kevin stood, and the .44's explosion echoed in the empty building. Robby fired twice more. The gun slammed his wrists like Donny'd warned, but it wasn't as bad as he expected. Kevin fired again, but the Uzi didn't stop.

"I can't hit nuthin' from here!" Kevin bawled. "C'mon!" He shoved past Robby and was out the door running when T.C.'s Uzi clacked empty. T.C. twisted around, grabbing on the seat for another clip, but forgetting to pull his spent one first. Robby scrambled to his feet, following Kevin, seeing T.C. yank the empty clip and jam in the full one. Squeaker brought his Uzi up, but Randers was moving fast and he couldn't seem to aim it right. More bottles and a rock hit the car. Squeaker fired, full-auto, swinging the gun like an exterminator spraying bugs. Robby saw Randers go down hard and his board skitter away. Robby fired at T.C. as the boy swung his Uzi toward Kevin. Rocks and bottles seemed to be raining out of the fog now. One hit Squeaker on the arm and he almost dropped the gun.

"Down!" Kevin yelled, as T.C. fired.

Kevin went flat to his chest, skidding through gravel and glass, arms out in front, hands locked on the .44's grip. Robby dropped too, feeling skin shred from his elbows while bullets cut the air overhead. *So that's what they really sounded like!* flashed through Robby's mind. It wasn't anything like TV when bullets were aimed at you! Robby fumbled the .45 toward T.C., broken glass slicing at his arms and chest. T.C. was fighting to hold the Uzi down, its muzzle trying to climb with each burst of fire, bullets sputting the building's concrete, some even raking splinters from the roof.

Kevin's .44 blasted again. It seemed to be the only gun that made a movie kind of sound. Robby jerked the .45's trigger until the slide clicked back empty. The .44 boomed twice more.

There was a kid-scream and T.C.'s Uzi cut off, clattering like a tin toy as it hit the pavement. T.C. seemed to just sit slowly down against the 'Vette's open door. His face looked surprised. A bottle crashed close to Robby and glass shards stung his cheek. He struggled up, almost slipping in the gravel. Jeez! How could three kids throw that much stuff. He saw a chunk of concrete lob from the night and slam into Squeaker's shoulder. Squeaker staggered, catching himself on the door but dropping the gun.

"Get him!" Kevin bawled, darting for the car. Robby yanked out the empty clip, feeling his knees and elbows burning in the chill air. He shoved in the full one and jerked up his head. There was Randers! He was up and running for Squeaker too. Squeaker saw him and grabbed for the Uzi. Robby brought his gun up, but Kevin was in the goddamn way. "Move, asshole!" Robby screamed. Randers would never get to Squeaker in time!

Suddenly, there were little orange flashes from Randers' shadowy form, and a popping sound like firecrackers. Squeaker screamed and dropped to the concrete, twisting and slapping at himself like there were yellowjackets stinging him.

Robby caught up to Kevin, and they rounded the front of the car in time to see Randers shove another clip into his little gun and aim down at Squeaker. All the time, Squeaker was screaming and begging and trying to crawl away. Though Robby's ears were still numb, he wanted to cover them. He'd barely heard Kevin's yells, but Squeaker's screaming seemed to beat right through to his brain. Robby's Pumas skidded in gravel and glass as he stopped behind Kevin and stared down at Squeaker. The rocks and bottles weren't falling anymore, and Robby heard shouts, but he couldn't take his eyes off Squeaker.

This wasn't like anything on TV. Dudes who got shot were supposed to be dead and still, not screaming and crawling. Robby remembered a dog in Fresno, hit by a car, flopping around in the street and screaming dog screams. You could feel the dog's agony and fear. This was worse. A zillion times worse. This was a boy!

Blood smell burned Robby's nose, sharp and coppery like new pennies. Dimly, he heard rattles and running feet, and small shadows darted from the fog. Two rode boards. Whitey, panting, carried his, a bottle still in the other hand. Randers' little gun popped again, but Squeaker only jerked as the bullets hit him . . . still moving, screaming, begging, "Don't, man, *please!*" over and over.

Kevin shook his head like he was trying to clear it, then aimed the .44 at Squeaker's back and pulled the trigger. The big hammer clanked down on nothing. Rix and Weasel rolled up and tailed, spraying gravel against the car's headlights and grill. Their eyes were wide, and Robby thought of that movie word "horror." Robby seemed to see things in a dream, like being stoned, where everything was fuzzy at the edges. Things seemed only half real. "Horror" was a word you saw on posters, not a look on kids' faces. Randers' gun was empty, and Squeaker wasn't dead, and the screaming wouldn't stop.

Robby couldn't think anymore. He wanted to run away, but there was nowhere to go. He dropped suddenly beside Squeaker, jammed the .45 against the back of the boy's head, and shot the gun empty. Blood spattered hot all over him, seeming to scald his arms and face.

There was no more screaming, except the echo of it in Robby's ears. Squeaker's body trembled for a few seconds. The dog had done that too.

For a long time there was silence. Robby stood up, still hearing the screams somewhere inside his head. The gun hung loose in his hand, both it and his arms dripping blood, the front of his shirt wet with it. He tasted Squeaker's blood on his lips. The silence of the other boys was almost like when some dude told a joke that was way too gross to be funny. Robby felt like that dude.

Then, Randers' head lifted, his eyes hard and clear. "Don't touch nuthin', *nobody!*" He shot glances all around. "Robby! Find you empty clip. Now! Rix! Gimme you shirt. Move!"

Rix looked away from Squeaker and yanked off his shirt. Randers grabbed it, spread it on the concrete, and dropped the Bersa and its other clip on it. He snagged the .44 from Kevin, then the .45 from Robby as he came back with the second clip. Randers started to tie a bundle.

"No!" Robby said. "Use mine!" He tore off his bloody shirt, almost ripping it to get it off his body.

Randers gave a short nod, tying the guns up in the blood-soaked tee and tossing it to Rix. "Run this down to the wharf. Throw it out far as you fuckin' can. Make sure no wino or nobody see. Book!"

Rix darted away, his dark body melting into the foggy night. Randers looked around again, cocking his head and listening hard, but there was only muffled quiet of fog. "Weasel! Take Rix's shirt. Snag the other Uzi an' any clips you can find. Whitey! Help him. Don't touch nuthin' else!" Randers snatched up Squeaker's Uzi while Weasel and Whitey moved around the front of the car.

"Hey!" came Weasel's yell. "Calvin's still alive!"

Robby, Randers, and Kevin ran to the other side of the 'Vette. T.C. lay back against the door, arms loose at his sides, legs sprawled out. There was blood all over his chest, flowing down and soaking his jeans, glistening black in reflected headlight glow. He looked up at the other boys. His eyes didn't seem scared or hurt, just confused. He was trying to breathe, but blood came out of his mouth, and Robby saw that it was choking him.

Robby shoved between Whitey and Weasel and knelt beside T.C. The blood smell made his own mouth salty. T.C. didn't even look thirteen now, more like ten, more like a little boy who'd gotten hurt playing with bigger boys. T.C.'s eyes met Robby's and seemed to look a question. He reached out his hand. Robby took it, warm and small, and started to stroke T.C.'s forehead. He watched the boy's eyes. They changed. It was like there just wasn't anything in them anymore. That was how the dog's eyes had looked.

Robby held the warm hand. He turned and looked up at Randers. "He's dead."

Wolf-Boy

THE hallway was dark, smelling of dust and rot and old piss, with webs in corners where spiders waited. The walls were splintered and scarred and so spray-painted it was hard to tell what color they might've been. Robby, carrying his board and following Slimer, glanced up at the dim ceiling. There were sockets, but no bulbs in them. He didn't even want to think about how the building would be at night. He hung back a few paces, watching Slimer. Maybe this was some kind of Rat ambush? How could anybody really be living in a place like this?

A little sun glow came from the stairwell behind and a dirty skylight toward the far end. The building was dead still and seemed deserted, traffic in the street and pigeons cooing somewhere above the only sounds. Slimer passed under the skylight. It was cracked, and he slipped in bird shit. "Fuckin' wind-rats!"

Slimer grinned back at Robby and pointed up. "Victor gots this old Daisy BB gun. Sometime kill some then eat. Eric cook."

"Yeah?" said Robby, still not sure what to believe. "What about them seagulls? They're bigger."

"Aw, yuk total they taste."

Slimer was supposed to be Robby's bodyguard in Ratland. At least that's what he said he'd be, back at the center when Robby had asked him about Eric. Robby had talked a little to Slimer before; the dude was friendly but hard to understand. Normally, Slimer didn't say much to anybody except Eric and Nathaniel, but if you acted at all as if you liked him, he'd start chattering away like a cracked-out first grader. Maybe there was a lot in his head, but it never seemed to come out right. Donny said he was a retard—twelve and couldn't even print his own name. Kevin said his mom had been on something when she'd had him. Even the other Rats called him stupid all the time, except Eric. Robby wasn't sure exactly why, but he wanted to meet Eric, and Slimer had offered to take him. Donny had looked doubtful about Robby going into Ratland, though Randers didn't seem surprised at all.

Slimer didn't look like much of a bodyguard. He was small and thin with a face that reminded Robby of those elves in Ireland. He was a strange kind of dusky color that looked dirty, and he *was* dirty all the time. It was hard to tell if he wore dreads on purpose or just never had his hair cut in his life. His jeans were ragged and ripped and way too small, and his faded black T-shirt and battered Nikes probably would've fit Nathaniel. He rode an ancient flat Variflex, tiger-stripped and thrashed to the max. Still, he seemed to laugh a lot, and his funny eyes—one blue, one brown—had a way of sparkling when he smiled.

Robby heard faint rap music as they neared a door. "Hot sounds."

Slimer nodded. "Or what. Eric's tape that be. Call 'By All Means Necessary.' BDP. Good rap. Tell you stuff 'sides shootin' an' killin' an' fuckin' bitches. Eric like it total. Go not with lunch two whole weeks to score. Me say I roust outa store for him, no prob. But no, say he." Slimer shrugged. "Eric that way."

They stopped at the door. There was a big brass number 13 on it, and Robby pointed down the hall. "Um, them other doors only say one an' two."

Slimer smiled. "Eric do that. Score he from spooky old hotel they wreckin'. Thing funny, hotel not gots room thirteen either, but Eric

126

snag a one an' a three." He stood on tiptoes, tracing the tarnished numbers with his finger. "One an' three, that together make thirteen, see?" He giggled. "Landlady don't much like, but Eric tell she this his door, pay for it, do fuckin' well what he want! Lady mega-old, ascared be of Eric. Figure he demon-boy. Be super nice to him, other way maybe he curse her."

"So, you mean Eric's got his *own* place?"

"Sorta. That he mom's 'partment next. This not real 'partment, see? Only little room used be somethin' else way long time pass. Chimney an' pipes go up in there. Mega-hot. Like hell. Nobody want for nuthin'. Eric pay own money, thirty buck a month. Do what he fuckin' want. Werewoofs like that." Slimer pushed Robby back. "Wait."

Slimer stood off to one side and knocked. The rap cut. Suddenly, there was a pop and splinters flew from the door panel. Slimer giggled and danced. "Miss me, miss me!"

Inside, a kid-voice swore. "Oh, shit! I'm sorry, man!"

Locks clacked and the door swung back to blackness. Its hinges creaked just the way Robby'd half expected them to. Heat seemed to pour into the hall as Eric looked out. He wore only ragged gray gym shorts, ripped up the side seams, leaving his thighs bare like an Indian boy in a movie. The heavy Rat chain rattled on his left ankle and a sloppy rolled cigarette dangled from his thin lips, smelling only of tobacco. He held a small rusty .22 in one long-fingered hand, pointed down. "Motherfuckin' thing goes off you just *breathe* on it anymore!"

Slimer grinned. "I know that gonna happen. I know it, man."

Eric smiled, halfway out the door, his wiry body glistening with sweat. He saw Robby and gave him a curious knowing look. "I knew I'd meet you, dude."

Robby studied Eric. "Um, you really a werewolf, man?"

Eric came close. His large eyes were totally black like there was no bottom to them. Robby tried, but he couldn't meet them for long. Eric smiled a funny kind of V smile. "Mmm. What you figure, Robby? Robby from Fresno. Rob-man." Eric's smile widened to show teeth that seemed too big somehow. "Grapes come from Fresno. Make California Raisins."

Robby took a step back. "Um, I guess you could be."

127

Eric grinned, and his teeth gleamed in the dimness. He moved close again, and Robby went suddenly still. Eric was a head taller, and Robby had to look up trying to read those eyes. Eric touched Robby's chest and it was like electricity sparked. Robby flinched back.

"Stop that!" Slimer yelled. "Robby just kill two dudes! Why you try an' scare him for?"

Eric closed his lips, though the strange smile stayed. "I not be scarin' Robby. He a Animal. Animals bad. I just testin' his aura. Tastin' kinda."

Slimer shoved between Eric and Robby. "Other Rats here?"

Eric still held Robby's eyes. "Kill. Meanin' to de-prive of life." His smile faded. "Tell you one thing, dude. Around here it don't matter if the bullets be silver or not." He glanced at Slimer. "No. Mason an' Victor out tryin' to make us some buck somehow. That why I can't figure who be knockin'."

Eric gazed in Robby's eyes again. "Why you be sad, man?"

Robby looked down, but Eric tilted his face up again. "Squeaker an' T.C.?"

"Mostly T.C."

"Mmm. There was no other way, Robby. You never forget that, long's you be livin'. You did what you had to do. An' it was a *good* thing. Maybe you not believe that now an' maybe this world call it bad. But good things matter, man. Not here, but somewhere."

Robby's eyes suddenly filled with tears. Eric smiled again. He wiped Robby's cheek then touched his finger to his own lips. "Feel my heart."

Robby hesitated, then put his palm to Eric's chest.

"*There* it matter." Eric's smile faded again and he looked sad. He stepped back and pointed to the doorway. "Aw, get the fuck inside before somebody come." He turned away, but Robby took his arm. "Is T.C. pissed at me?"

"No. You hold his hand when he die. One second he not lonely no more."

"Yeah?" said Slimer. "Bet Squeaker pissed!"

Robby tensed, but Eric only shrugged. "Squeaker where he belong, man. *For*-ever!"

They moved to the doorway, but Eric turned again and put his hand

128

on Robby's chest. "Aw, I ain't thinkin', dude. Sorry. I ain't on nuthin', but this door's a gate and crazy-boy Slimer rattle it. Break my journey. Figure I got to search you. For silver bullets." He smiled again, keeping the gun pointed away.

Robby shrugged and yanked off his shirt, spreading his arms and turning slow. Slimer did the same and Eric gave him a disgusted look. "Not you, crazy-boy."

"Aw, I just hot," said Slimer. He grinned and pointed at Robby. "Jeans too!"

Robby flushed and dropped his hand to the buttons. Eric gave him another smile. "That's cool, dude. Don't need to see your dick." He melted into the hot darkness, his voice calling back. "Assume your doom when you enter this room."

Slimer eased close to Robby and whispered. "Gots a hard, don't 'cha?"

Robby sighed, sweat on his face. "Uh huh."

Slimer grinned. "Eric not homo . . . sleep I with him lotsa times. But he make you feel like one, like you wanna touch him. Be close. That his woof-magic, man. His au-ra. One time, big dude at school try an' get Eric in the bathroom for homo stuff. Day next, dude dead. Dirt-nap time."

"Eric killed him?"

"Maybe not how you figure. Dude some bad rock score. OD." Slimer looked cheerful. "But, believe it, Eric kill him just the same. Woof-curse, see?"

Robby and Slimer came into the little room. Slimer closed the door. Robby felt fear for a moment because there was only blackness and a ghostly green glow. Then his eyes began to adjust and he saw the faint light came from a stereo dial. Gradually, he made out a mattress on the floor against the far wall, a deep-sink with a two-burner hot plate on a shelf stove, and an ancient fridge painted black. Somehow you never imagined a black fridge. Against the other wall were some rough boards on bricks with a lot of books on them. In the middle of the room was a wooden table and two chairs. A huge brick chimney rose through the floor and ceiling, radiating heat, and there were a lot of pipes overhead. A single bulb dangled from wires over the table.

Eric was suddenly beside Robby, and Robby almost jumped. Eric touched his board. "Hot old Steadham, dude. You all ride bullets in raisin-land?"

"Um. Oh." Robby shrugged, relaxing a little. "You know what it is, all dudes run the same. Kevin let me ride his board once. He gots old Kryptonics, seventies. They run better on rough stuff than anything I ever seen. Too bad they don't make 'em no more, but Kevin's gonna find me a set." It didn't seem scary talking to Eric about boards.

Eric nodded. "You like Kevin, huh?"

"For sure."

"That good. Kevin need somebody like you to like him."

Slimer walked over near the mattress. "Robby-dude! You gotta check out Eric's board. It somethin' total else!"

Eric grinned, snapping the door locks and waving a hand. "For sure. Check it."

Robby edged away a little and Eric's teeth flashed once more. "Aw, don't be scared, man. Touch me if you want. I know what you feel."

Robby looked at the floor. "Um, you mean you can read my mind?"

Eric laughed, a good laugh. "That wouldn't be cool. In-vade your privacy."

"But, um, you could?"

Slimer, sitting on the mattress, giggled. "Or what! An' you should be 'shamed!"

Robby flushed, glad of the darkness, but Eric only squatted and peered through the bullet hole. "Fuck! Maybe the landlady not see?"

"She see," laughed Slimer. "You mom she tell! Get you skinny ass spanked!"

Eric stood, pulling the gun's clip and carefully jacking out the bullet. "Aw, I'll tell her I shot at a junkie or somethin'."

Slimer nodded. "Good idea."

Robby's eyes were used to the dimness now and he checked around again. There were a lot of pictures and posters on the walls—some skate stuff, heavy-metal and rap groups, ghosts, demons, the Ninja Turtles, and a really scary one of the Reaper with his huge bright blade. The room smelled mostly of cigarettes and Eric.

Slimer kicked out of his Nikes and pulled off his jeans, sitting cross-

130

legged and naked on the blankets. "Eric like the dark," he said. "Werewoofs do, see?" He spread both arms and waved around at the posters. "Eric into total scaaary shit. Sometime read me spooky stories, bones an' dirt-naps an' worm food. I get bad dreams."

Eric sat at the table and laid down the gun, shrugging. "Don't need light to listen to music. Cost extra anyways. 'Sides, I know what this dogshit place look like." He pointed to Slimer. "An' don't pay no attention to him. Don't know why I do most times. He crazy. Always be sayin' off the wall shit. 'Course sometime it make sense if you listen long enough."

"Yeah?" said Slimer. "Robby say that too."

Eric gazed over at Robby. "Mmm. Yeah, you would."

Slimer held up something shiny. "Check this, Robby."

Robby came over and took it—an ancient aluminum board, long and narrow, with a wicked-looking nose, pointed and sharp.

"Eric build that," said Slimer. "Score deck in dumpster with them funny old ACS trucks. Put on Rat-Bones, rails, an' Bird. Eric make it do stuff *nobody* do on regular boards, 'cause of woof-magic, see? Say it be like Sword of Omen for Lion-o. Cut the shit outa some big asshole dude with the nose one time."

Robby touched the board's nose. "Or what!" He checked the board carefully. "This is totally hot! Never seen nuthin' like it before. Musta been some bad kids rode these in the old days."

Eric shrugged, but smiled. "Aw, there be a lot of stuff you can't do on it, no kick-tail. But I like it. Sometime you shouldn't give a fuck what the other dudes do. When you figure somethin's right for you, go for it."

Robby thought for a moment, then nodded. "Yeah. Um, you think, sometime, I could ride it?"

Eric smiled wider. "For sure, raisin-boy." His teeth glinted. "If we don't got to kill you." He struck a match with his thumbnail. Robby blinked in the sudden flare, then jumped back from the table. *Shit!*"

There was a skull on the table, a small skull.

Eric still grinned, lighting a candle on top of the skull. "This's Trevor, man. What be left of him. Look a little different with his skin off, huh? Used to be a evil dude—like Squeaker. Put a lot of kids in

131

hell." Eric laughed again, but a scary laugh this time. "Now Trevor in real hell. *For*-ever!"

Robby leaned close and peered at the skull. "Um, where—"

"Don't *even* ask!" said Slimer.

Eric nodded, flicking the skull with his finger, making a dry thunk. "Figure I score Squeaker's too, in a while." He stretched and glanced around. "Oh, hope you dudes ain't hungry. Got zip, as usual."

Robby was still staring at the skull. "You're not gonna get T.C.'s, are you?"

Eric picked up the skull and gazed into the empty eye sockets. "T.C. in peace, man. Not bother him. Maybe somewhere, sometime, he get another chance. Universe a big place. Big enough to work everythin' out in the end, maybe."

"Oh!" said Slimer. He reached for his jeans and dug in the pocket, pulling out something wrapped in foil. "Brung you a egg-a-muffin, sorta. Robby make at Donny's. Squished a little." He tossed it to Eric.

Eric held it to his nose. "Mmm. Smells good." He looked up at Robby. "Thanks. Offerin's always 'ppreciated."

Slimer clapped his hands. "Yeah! Now you gotta do magic for Robby."

"He already did, kinda," said Robby.

Eric smiled around a mouthful, beckoning Robby close with a long finger. He waved his hand, empty, then reached behind Robby's ear and came up with a nickel.

"Hey!" said Robby. "That's hot, man!"

Slimer giggled. "Sometime it a quarter."

"I put it back," said Eric, showing Robby his hand, empty again. "Maybe it get to be a quarter. Good dude like you worth a quarter."

Robby touched his ear. "Um, where's it go?"

"Where everythin' go, what ain't here no more."

"Oh."

Slimer suddenly scooted off the mattress and yanked a book from a shelf. "Check this, Robby-dude! Eric read *real* books, see? No pitchers even!"

Eric smiled, tearing at the sandwich with his big teeth. "Aw, crazy-boy, stop fuckin' with my stuff."

Robby went over and took the book from Slimer. "Hey, this is real!" He studied the cover and traced a few sentences with his finger, frowning in concentration and moving his lips. Slimer watched him, fascinated. Finally, Robby looked back at Eric. "This's a hard book, man. I figure even Donny'd have a hassle with it. Fuck, you must be mega-smart."

Eric shrugged, though his eyes sparkled. "Nuthin' else to do. Can't make magic on dope an' crackers. Got no TV, junkie roust it. He didn't want my blaster 'cause it's total dogshit. I score books at the Center sometimes. Leese brings 'em, Alpo too. He okay for a homo. Even plays D an' D."

Robby slipped the book back with the others. "Um, figure, sometime, you'd read to me? If I bring you somethin'?"

Eric grinned around the last mouthful. "For sure, Robby-dude. An' you don't gotta bring nuthin' but your mind." He glanced at the skull once more. " 'Course, Mason might not like a Animal comin' into Ratland, y'know?"

Slimer stood up. "Mason go fuck his ownself! Mason hurt Robby Animal-friend, I kill him!"

Eric sighed. "Oh, shut up. Somebody kill you soon enough, crazy-boy." He flicked the skull again and sighed. "I howl over your grave. Maybe keep you here with me."

Slimer spat on the floor. "No way! Not aside Trevor-asshole!"

Robby sat in the other chair, looking at Eric over the candle-glow. "Um," he said, voice low. "Some of the dudes say you can see things—like the future." He flicked his eyes toward Slimer. "Um, you don't mean . . . "

Eric frowned a little. "Sometimes it's better just not to look." He sighed again, as Slimer sat back down and checked the aluminum board once more. "See Slimer in your mind, two year, three year from now. Always he be a little kid, only he be too big to be one no more." He shrugged. "You an' me, we *old* kids already, man, startin' to get where kid stuff don't make us happy. All kids go through them changes, even squid-kids, only they know they goin' somewhere. But we nuthin', man. We goin' nowhere. Squids won't *let* us go nowhere. Maybe they scared of us—somethin' I not figured yet. But that feelin' make dudes crazy. Like your Kevin. Now, Randers, he different, even if he don't know it. Maybe keepin' Animals together keep him together? You cool, too, in a different way. Maybe you live to get outa here, you be a cool big dude." He flicked the skull again. "When you go back to Fresno, take Kevin with you, somehow, man. There's ways kids can make it without no big people helpin' long's they got friends like you."

Robby frowned. "I ain't never goin' back there!"

Eric shrugged. "Maybe, maybe not."

"Um, could you look?"

"Don't work that way. Ain't a goddamn TV, dude. What I see mostly only what *could* happen 'less somethin' change. We make our own futures, raisin-boy. If we couldn't, the whole universe just be jackin' itself off." He grinned. "You don't understand that, do you?"

"Uh uh."

"Mmm. I think you will. Just remember, shit happens." Eric's eyes cooled a little. "That the only reason you come here, man? Ask about T.C. an' try to get your stupid fortune told?"

Slimer jumped up and pointed to Eric. "Why you be a scrote now?" He came over and put his hand on Robby's shoulder. "You say just Robby be a good dude, an' Randers too! Maybe be time for Rats an' Animals be good dudes all together? Maybe no more dead kids, see? Even stupid Mason gotta hear that."

Eric was quiet awhile, licking his fingers. "Mmm." He gave Robby a smile. "What I tell you about Slimer, man? Listen long enough an' he make a kind of sense. Somebody else soon be takin' Squeaker's place. Always happen."

"Animals got two Uzi's!" said Slimer.

Eric shrugged. "Figured they'd have to go somewhere, not like the nickel."

"Well," said Robby. "Um, maybe the Rats an' Animals could kinda talk, y'know?" He considered. "Maybe Nathaniel'd let us use his room some night?"

Eric gazed at the skull, then nodded slowly. "Kids got good minds." He thought a few moments more. "Mmm. Maybe somethin' could happen."

"Make it happen, man!" said Slimer. "With woof-magic!"

"Hey, crazy-boy. If wolf magic could make the world better, there wouldn't be no more probs at all."

Slimer shrugged. "Maybe there just ain't enough werewoofs?"

Eric laughed. "That's my homey!" He looked back at Robby. "Stupid for Rats an' Animals to fight. Ain't nuthin' here worth fightin' over anyways. This might be a good thing, man. I think Mason'll hear."

Slimer threw himself back on the mattress and stretched out, giggling, arms under his head. "Robby-dude! What Eric say, mean really he talk for Rats. Mason only *think* he do, see?"

Eric grinned and stood up. "Wanna hear my tape, Robby?"

"For sure. An', after, could you read me some stuff?"

"Yeah!" said Slimer. "An' do some more magic for Robby too!"

Dream

"RANDERS wipin' some squid's ass by the big fish!"

Nathaniel dropped his cigarette and stomped it. "Aw, dogshit!"

He ran after Whitey, who was panting hard. Behind came Weasel and Rix. People parted fast to let them through. Nathaniel, leading now, ragged and dirty as the kids, looked pissed as hell.

It was almost over by the dolphin tank anyway. There were two white squid-kids about sixteen. One was a total marshmallow, in baggies, Airwalks, and David Lee Roth T-shirt. He had a pot belly and a bloody nose. Nathaniel shoved between a couple of watching kids in time to see Randers give the other squid an industrial-strength kick in the balls. The big dude doubled and puked. Randers wasn't even breathing hard. Nathaniel glanced around. Robby and Kevin stood over by the dolphin tank. A lot of adults were looking disgusted and dragging their little kids away. There were some shouted "All rights" from bigger kids, and Kevin flashed a raised thumb at Randers while the other Animals crowded around him grinning.

136

Nathaniel sighed. "Showtime's over, dudes."

A few old people were still muttering and shaking their heads while puke-stink drifted above the smells of clean saltwater and hot concrete. Nathaniel tapped Rix on the shoulder. "Watch for rattlers, man."

Rix nodded and stood on tip-toes looking around. Everybody was moving away now, except a couple of black kids on a bench who were sharing a big Coke and still grinning.

"Where's Donny?" Nathaniel asked.

Weasel pointed. "Gettin' a hot dog or somethin'."

Nathaniel nodded. "Yeah, right. You dudes seen enough fish today?"

"Yeah," said Whitey, firing a Marlboro. "It was hot!"

Weasel pulled at Nathaniel's arm. "Hey! Figure we can stop at McDonald's on the way back, man?"

"Why? You wanna fish sandwich?" asked Rix.

"No way," said Whitey. "They probably make 'em outa all the fish what croak here."

"Fuck you, man!" said Weasel. "Do not."

"Shut up," said Randers.

Nathaniel glanced over where Kevin and Robby were watching the dolphins play, standing close, heads almost touching, talking and smoking. The two squids left, bloody-nose helping the other, ignored by the Animals, snickered at by the kids on the bench, stared at by everybody else. Nathaniel raised one eyebrow at Randers.

Randers shrugged. "Assholes was hasslin' Kevin an' Robby, man. Makin' jokes about niggers an' skate-punks. Make fun of them fish too, an' Robby likes to watch 'em, total."

Nathaniel looked back at Robby and Kevin who seemed fascinated by the dolphins.

"They real pretty," said Randers. "Kinda black an' white, an' all shiny an' friendly."

Nathaniel smiled and nodded. "Yeah. I hear. Um, you wanna take the dudes back to the van? I'll wait here for Donny."

"Yeah," said Randers. "He cupped his hands to his mouth and bawled, "Yo, Robby, Kevin."

Kevin turned around, but Robby still watched the dolphins.

137

"Maybe I could talk to Robby while I'm waitin'," said Nathaniel.

Randers grinned. "Yeah. That'd be cool. See you at the van, man."

The kids left in a wedge, Randers leading. People let them through, no prob.

Robby glanced up as Nathaniel came over, but Nathaniel only leaned on the rail and fired a cigarette. "Want one, man?"

"Yeah," said Robby. "Thanks." He blew smoke and pointed to the dolphins. "Um, how come they got those holes in their heads?"

"That's the way they breathe."

Robby studied Nathaniel's face a second. "I didn't know fish could breathe."

Nathaniel smiled. "Well, they ain't really fish. Fish are stupid. *They* don't look stupid, do they?"

"No way! I can see that. It's like they get to play all the time, y'know?"

"Yeah. Some of them science doctors even figure they're smarter than people."

Robby giggled. "I can see that. They ain't fightin'." He turned back to the tank, gazing at the playing dolphins. "They're like water dudes, huh?"

"For sure."

Robby sighed. "Sometimes I still wanna just play too." He looked up at Nathaniel. "Um, does that sound like baby shit, man?"

"No." Nathaniel let smoke out through his nose and watched the dolphins. "You ever want to go home or just talk to somebody, you know where I am, okay?"

Robby nodded, then looked up again. "Um, how come you're not tryin' to make me go back?"

"Would you stay?"

"I don't think so. I mean, who wants to get stuck in a foster home?"

Nathaniel shrugged. "They're not *all* dogshit. I grew up in one. It wasn't that bad. Some of the people who run 'em really do like kids."

"Yeah?"

Nathaniel smiled. "Straight-up." He glanced over as Donny came over, then turned to Robby again. "Anyways, you know where I'm at."

Robby nodded, watching the dolphins once more. Nathaniel touched his shoulder. "Gotta go, man. Sorry."

The old van was in the back corner of the parking lot. Letters on the front used to say DODGE, but some Center kids had screwed with them, and now they spelled DOG.

It had a flat tire.

"Dogshit!" said Nathaniel.

Randers tapped Whitey on the shoulder. "Get the jack." He turned to Rix. "Help him."

Kevin came close to Robby and whispered, "Nathaniel's cool, huh?"

"Or what."

Donny climbed in the front of the van, flipping on the radio. Iron Maiden blasted out.

"Ain't no fuckin' jack, man!" Whitey bawled from the back.

The other Animals glanced at each other, then to Randers and Nathaniel. Kevin gave Robby a nudge in the ribs, smiled, and walked off.

Robby looked at the flat. "Um, maybe we could all lift it or somethin'?"

Whitey glared out of the side door. "Ain't no good anyways. Some asshole rousted the fuckin' wrench thing too."

Randers looked at Nathaniel. "Somebody gonna get they ass wiped."

Nathaniel smiled, then climbed in back with Whitey, digging under the seats, through empty Coke cans and Burger King boxes. "Aw, maybe it's under all this shit." He laughed. "Be a long fuckin' ride back to Oakland on the boards."

The kids grinned and snickered. "Um, figure they make us pay bridge toll there at Martinez?" giggled Weasel.

"Shut up," said Randers. He climbed in back with Nathaniel and started shoving stuff around.

Robby saw Kevin coming back, grinning. He held up a shiny red scissors jack and a chrome star wrench. "These work, man?" he asked Nathaniel.

Nathaniel slid out and took them. The jack said "Toyota" on it. "Or what. Thanks, dude."

Randers poked his head out and gave Kevin a nod. "Put 'em back when we done."

"Yeah." Kevin fired a cigarette, and touched Robby's shoulder. "Um, let's get the spare, okay?"

"I'm hungry," said Donny. "We gonna stop at McDonald's?"

"Gotta fix the tire first, lame-o," yelled Whitey.

"Bucks," said Randers. He held out his hand. The others dug in their pockets, including Nathaniel. Randers counted the money. "Yeah. We gots enough for that."

"Quarter pounders?" asked Rix.

"With cheese?" asked Weasel.

Randers smiled a little and nodded. "Maybe even small fries."

Robby giggled. "Um, guess that's being nigger-rich, huh?"

The kids broke up. "Hey," yelled Weasel, "I was gonna say that."

"You snooze, you lose, man," said Kevin.

Randers came over to Robby. "Wanna stay at my place tonight, man?"

"For sure."

Whitey and Rix changed the tire. Nathaniel let the jack down and handed it to Kevin. Kevin decked and rolled off between the cars. The others piled in the van, Randers up front with Nathaniel. Robby stood in the open side door, gazing back toward Marine World.

"What'er you thinkin', man?" asked Donny.

"Aw, about them dolphins. They sure look happy."

"I wish you wouldn't drink beer," said Randers' mom.

Randers shut the fridge, handing Robby a Bud. "Aw, it only one, Mom. Make me an' Robby sleep better. Sometime we think too much."

Randers' mom smiled a little and got her sweater off its hook by the door. "What's Robby's mom think about that?"

"Aw, it's cool," said Robby. "Long's it's only one."

Randers' mom smiled again. "Okay, boys. But just that one." She sighed, glancing toward the window. " 'Spose it's a little late for all that, 'be smart, don't start,' stuff around here, huh?"

Randers smiled, standing on tiptoes to kiss her. "Or what, Mom."

She reached over and ruffled Robby's hair, then looked at Randers again. "Well, I gonna be all right, son. They some kinda strike talk at the hospital again. Don't never got enough nurses there anyway."

Robby studied her. She was nice. Her white uniform smelled like doctor stuff.

Randers took a sip of beer. "When you get to be a real nurse, Mom?"

She laughed and chucked Randers under the chin. "Take money to live, boy. Even you always tellin' me that. Nobody pay you for goin' to classes." She smiled at Robby again, then stopped at the door, looking at her son. "How was Marineworld, honey?"

"Total hot! Maybe we go there sometime?"

"Yeah!" said Robby. "They got these dolphins. Just watchin' 'em makes you feel good."

Randers' mom smiled at the boys. "Maybe someday, son, when I can get the time." She gave Robby a wink. "My boy know how to pick good friends. I see that."

"Aw, Mom!" Randers said.

She smiled wider. "I'm leavin'. Lock the door, an' don't stay up too late." She glanced back. "An' *don't* be smokin' in bed."

Randers grinned at Robby as he snapped the two locks behind her. "She always say that."

Robby smiled. "You got a super cool mom."

Randers nodded, pulling off his shirt and kicking out of his Cheetahs. "Yeah. She see a lot of shit at that hospital. She know what is, believe it." He turned off the light and stretched. "Want a smoke before we go to bed?"

Robby chugged his beer. "Naw. thanks, Randers. Guess I'm kinda tired."

Randers yawned. "Yeah. Me too." He killed his Bud, took Robby's empty, and dropped them in a paper bag under the sink. They lay down together on the mattress by the window, and Randers pulled the blanket over them. "Night, dude."

141

"Night."

Robby lay awake a little while listening to Randers' steady breathing. He'd gone to sleep right away. It had to take a lot of energy to keep a gang together Robby thought. It must be like having to think for five other dudes besides yourself. Robby wondered if Randers ever got a chance to play in his life. The air was still warm and the window was open, streetlight shining in. There were smells of tar and exhaust and he could hear traffic on 880. He moved a little closer to Randers and closed his eyes.

Robby stood against the side of the tank, chest-deep in green water. He wore only jeans and the big dog-choker Kevin had given him around his neck. The sky was clear and blue above, and there were green hills in the distance. But the colors seemed to mean something different to his mind.

The green was like shallow water, and the blue—the blue was best, because it reminded him of the deep indigo that shaded even darker as you dove down through until finally it became like the blue-black of his brother's skin.

Robby thought these thoughts in a daylight dream, clearer than acid, cleaner than dust—good thoughts that no drug could bring. Slowly, his eyes returned to the upper world. He drifted past a door, though he didn't want to, hearing it close behind him in his mind.

He pulled himself from the tank and sat awhile, paddling his feet in the cool water. He was confused. There were two worlds in his mind. His brother would know. His brother could explain it. Where was his brother?

The sun seemed suddenly hot on his back, and he slid into the water again. He walked slowly across, neck deep in the center, to the far side where concrete steps led up to a wide space. There was a big ugly wooden box. That was his home for awhile.

Robby sat on one of the steps, chest-deep in water. His dark body glistened in the sunlight. The rattle of a padlock and chain at the gate made him look. They were hard metal sounds that belonged to the upper world. Doctor Nathaniel came in, pale hair like gold in the sun. He was a boy and a man at the same time.

Doctor Nathaniel locked the gate again and walked around the tank. He carried the food dish, and had one of those doctor things for listening to hearts around his neck.

"What's up, Robby?" he asked.

Robby smiled and climbed out of the water, standing on sun-hot concrete, dripping a puddle at his feet. Doctor Nathaniel put the dish down and listened to Robby's heart. He was a cool dude. Robby's brother said so too.

"Them jeans are all wore out, man," Doctor Nathaniel said. "I could go up an' score you some new ones."

Robby shrugged. "I don't figure I'll need 'em soon."

Doctor Nathaniel gave Robby the food dish, then sat by the water. "How do you know what is?"

Robby smiled. "My brother told me." He ate the food with his fingers.

Doctor Nathaniel fired a cigarette and seemed to think about that. Robby had to stop eating once and go back in the water for a little while. It was quiet and nice. There were no car noises or exhaust stink. He put his head under and opened his eyes. The water was cool and clean, and he thought of his brother again, shiny and beautiful. He felt his brother near, somehow, and waited for the door to open. But, it didn't. He climbed back out of the water and sat beside Doctor Nathaniel.

"I wanna go home," Robby said.

Doctor Nathaniel gazed at the water and nodded. "I know. I do too." He put his hand on Robby's shoulder. "Are you scared, man?"

"Sometimes."

"Hey, you're cryin', dude!"

Robby smiled, watching his tears fall in the water, making little rings. "That's okay. My brother knows."

"Maybe it's too soon? Maybe you can't handle it yet."

Robby shrugged. "I was scared at first. It was like tryin' to swim; you're scared 'cause there's nuthin' to hang onto. You're all by yourself over blue deep. It was like that. Then, my brother came. He said, 'don't be scared, everything's cool.' Said I wouldn't be alone no more ..." Robby looked at Doctor Nathaniel. "I need to see him."

143

Doctor Nathaniel looked at Robby a long time. Then he nodded. He went to the box and came back with a rusty chain. He knelt and locked the chain to Robby's choker and held the other end. They walked to the gate and Doctor Nathaniel unlocked it. Then they went down a long concrete sidewalk between tall chain-link fences with rusty barbed wire on top. It was a long way and the sun was hot, but they came out on a white sandy beach.

There was no surf; only blue ripples lapping at the clean sand under a clear sky. Out in the water a dolphin played. It saw them and came close, looking at Robby with friendly beautiful eyes. Robby moved forward, but the chain held him back. He turned and smiled at Doctor Nathaniel. "It's cool. Really."

They walked to the water and sat in the shallows. The dolphin came right up, quiet and peaceful, while Robby stroked its glistening skin. The dolphin looked at him and said a word that Robby heard in his mind.

"It's time," said Robby.

Doctor Nathaniel looked sad.

"Um, you gonna cry?" asked Robby.

"Yeah."

Robby touched Doctor Nathaniel's arm. "Hey, it's totally cool. My brother's opening the door now."

Doctor Nathaniel nodded, then hugged Robby a long time. Then he unlocked the chain. Robby stood and walked into the sparkling ocean. The dolphin swam beside him. Robby stopped and looked back at the shore.

"I wish I was your brother," Doctor Nathaniel said.

Robby smiled and held out his hand. "You are."

Randers woke up in the late night stillness. Robby was pressed close to him, gripping his hand tight. Randers lay still, watching the curtains sway in the cool salt breeze. Then, he gently closed his own fingers over Robby's and lay that way a long time, staring at the ceiling until he fell asleep again.

Werewolf Night

WEREWOLF NIGHT. Fog drifted thick over rooftops. Sunday nights were best. No cars cruised below in streets like misty rivers. Traffic sound came muffled from 880—trucks mostly, diesel thunder, whine of big tires, distant and lonely.

Eric seemed to glide through mist swirls across glistening tarpaper. He reached a brick parapet and looked down. He wore only jeans, both knees ripped open, and huge old Cons held together by tape. The fog rolled in cold waves from the Bay, and waterdrops sparkled in Eric's bushy hair while his dark body glinted, but werewolves didn't need shirts.

The street below was empty, lights poking up, far apart, one dim and dying. The street was the line. This block was Rat ground; Animals on the other. The gangs were talking now at the Center, still wary, but beginning to wonder why gangs had to fight each other. Because the papers and TV said so? Street kids should be smarter than that. There were better things to fight than each other. Maybe kids killing kids gave the squid-world something to laugh about? Eric gazed across the street. Still, it was cool to get permission or at least have a good reason for crossing.

For Eric, that didn't matter much. He traveled above, while other kids rode their skateboards through dogshit. Sometimes Eric rode too, his strange old aluminum board that came from another time. But Eric liked the roofs better; werewolves always liked high dark places.

Up the block to his right was some kind of old factory, closed forever. A big rusty pipe spanned the street at third-story level. Kids walked it on a dare in daytime. Eric crossed at night, no prob.

He climbed the parapet, running along crumbling brick to the next building. It was lower, but an easy eight-foot drop. Inside was some kind of industrial laundry. Vans came and went twenty-four hours, though fewer on weekends. The air above smelled clean—hot soapy water and towel cloth like the locker room at school. Steam ghosted pale from tall stacks. Eric stopped at one, pressing his back to the warm iron, feeling the old .22 pistol jammed in his jeans. It wasn't much of a street gun; when cocked, you never knew if it would go off by itself. But a werewolf didn't need much of a gun, and any kid who knew Eric left him alone.

Nearby was a skylight, glowing blue-white from florescents below. The hum of machinery came faint and the roof thrummed underfoot. The skylight could be opened like a starship's airlock. Eric had prowled the clean empty corridors down there once. It was like the Enterprise on auto-pilot, panels glowing with colored lights and everything seeming to function fine without people around. Eric liked to pretend he was traveling warp-seven to another universe. He moved on.

The factory roof was ten feet higher, vast slopes of rusty tin that clattered and squeaked unless you knew where to walk. Eric climbed a pipe, crotch pressed to warm wet iron, loving it the way he imagined he'd love a girl someday, his cock throbbing hot by the time he reached the top. Stupid, he thought, getting turned on by a goddamn pipe, but it felt good anyway. "Asshole," he murmured, grinning. Did werewolves fuck, he wondered? Naw, dipshit, the goddamn *stork* brought Eddie Munster! He scrambled to the roof and moved up the slope toward the peak. If werewolves fucked, what form did they take? None of his books said anything about that. Of course none of his books had black werewolves or elves, but he always figured that was only because nobody had gotten around to writing about them yet.

This was the highest roof for blocks. He straddled the summit, leaning back, arms spread to the sky, gazing into soft blackness above. His cock was still hard and he felt like howling, but city werewolves had to be cool.

He ran along the ridge to the street end, then down, dropping to the pipe, worn soles slipping a little on the wet iron. Below, a laundry van rattled away, but Eric had discovered a long time ago that people never looked up. Eric crossed empty space, fast for any other kid, carefully for him. Werewolves weren't stupid, eighty feet to concrete was as good as a silver bullet any day. The other roof was flat. The pipe made a ninety and went through. Eric slid down in Animal-land.

Blocks away, he heard the sound of a car skidding around a corner and the rumble of twin pipes. Kid-car for sure, Mopar 360, maybe just a 318. It faded in the fog, headed over East. Shit always happened there, but that was another universe too. Here, maybe there wasn't much to see on late Sunday werewolf nights, but there were things Eric never wanted to see again, anywhere.

Sundays the dudes were in early. There was school in the morning; big dudes and old people had to work. Even the winos were quiet, like Sunday was still sort of special for them too. Yeah, nothing much happening, but it was a hot night to prowl.

Then he heard voices, kid-voices, cheerful and rowdy, and an old-lady voice, pissed as hell. Eric grinned again, running across the roofs to where an alley cut the block. He knew those voices—old Mrs. Thompson, the thrift-store lady who hated kids, especially skate-punk kids, and Rix, Robby, and Kevin. Showtime for sure on an Oakland werewolf night.

He reached the parapet, crouched, and peered over. The gun poked his butt so he laid it on the roof. Across the alley, a second-floor window was open and Mrs. Thompson leaned out. She looked like a badass Oprah Winfrey a long time off her diet. "I say stop all that goddamn noise you makin'!" she raged.

147

Below, the three boys stood together, each with a foot on his board. They were grinning and gazing up, hands on hips. Rix laughed. "Ain't no noise here, cow-lady! We rappin' that all. Rappin' be music. Music a good thing. What your music, Isaac Hayes?"

The Animals all snickered.

Mrs. Thompson shook a huge fist. "What you tellin' me, smart-ass little niggerboys!"

Eric leaned elbows on brick, chin in hands, and snickered too.

Below, the boys totally broke up. Rix and Robby both pointed to Kevin. Kevin grinned, spread his arms and took a bow. Robby called up, "Need glasses, old lady?"

Mrs. Thompson shook her fist again. "I come down there, I slap your teeth right down your throats. Yes I will!"

"Yeah?" bawled Kevin. "You an' who's army?"

"I call the goddamn cops!"

Kevin flipped her off. "Yeah? Try an' get 'em to even come, you old cow!"

Rix twisted around, dropped his jeans and gave her a moon. The window slammed.

The boys snickered and giggled, turning to each other, words carrying soft to Eric's ears. "Figure she do that?" asked Rix.

"Could happen," said Robby. "She's mega-pissed, or what!"

"Yeah," said Kevin. "An' she knows Rix's mom, too." He grinned. "She'll tell her an' you'll get your ass spanked, man."

Rix thought about that a moment, then shrugged and grinned too. "Oh well." He looked up the alley, "Aw, I gotta get home anyways."

"Me too, I guess," said Kevin. "My mom's been pretty cool lately."

"Maybe you bein' cooler to you mom?" Rix suggested.

Kevin frowned, but Robby grinned and punched his arm. "Kinda hot sometimes," Robby said, "knowin' there ain't nobody gives a shit if I ever get home or not."

Kevin punched him back. "Yeah? *We* give a shit, dude. You got six homes here, an' that ain't even countin' the Center."

"Yeah," said Rix. "Hey, you wanna sleep over with me tonight? It cool with my mom. She thinks you cuter even than Weasel."

"Naw, thanks anyway. I told Donny I'd be there tonight. Gotta get over before his mom comes home." He grinned. " 'Sides, you kick all the time."

"Yeah?" said Rix. "Well, you snore."

"Do not."

"Do," said Kevin. "Hey, you mean Donny's mom still ain't figured out you're stayin' there? I never thought she was dense, y'know?"

Robby shrugged. "Donny said he thinks she knows, but she's bein' cool. Anyhow, Donny eats so much that she never misses what he gives me."

Kevin grinned and patted Robby's stomach. "Yeah? Don't look like *you're* missin' anything neither, man. You're gettin' almost as fat as Whitey."

"Aw," said Rix. "Long's he don't get as fat as Donny, he be cool."

"Well," said Kevin. "You can stay with me if you want, or we could go up to the Center. Maybe Nathaniel gets lonely too."

Rix smiled. "Ever figure Nathaniel might want to have a lady in his bed, 'stead of some dirty smelly kid?"

Kevin cocked his head. "Fuck. Hey, y'know, I never even thought of that."

"Aw," said Robby. "It's cool, dudes. Thanks again. But you know Donny, he'll get all hyper an' start worryin' just like somebody's mommy or somethin'." He decked his board. "See ya. Think about me when you're stuck in school tomorrow."

Kevin grinned again. "Aw, eat shit an' die, asshole."

Rix and Kevin watched Robby roll down the alley, cutting around cans in the dark. "Too bad he never got to see the ocean," murmured Kevin.

Rix snagged his blaster off a dumpster lid. "Well, shit. We ain't never seen it neither." He rolled up the other way, Kevin following.

Above, Eric grabbed his gun, shoving it back in his jeans, and booked across the roofs. The little market on the corner had a concrete slab jutting out over its doorway and heavy iron rods angled up to hold it. Eric scrambled over the parapet and slid down a rod to the slab, already hearing Robby's Bullets clicking cracks along the sidewalk. Eric swung over the edge and dropped in front of Robby.

"Shit!" Robby yelled, tailing, skidding, and landing on his ass.

Eric grinned. "What's up, raisin-boy?"

Robby got up, rubbing his butt and frowning. "Not funny, man. Jeez. Hey, you know everything, can kids get heart attacks?"

Eric considered. "Mmm. Maybe."

"Yeah? Well, you almost gave me one. Fuck! I wanna live a little longer anyways."

"To see your ocean?"

"How did you know? Oh yeah, I keep forgettin'. 'Woof magic, see?"

Eric shrugged. "Death comes like that sometimes. Mr. Reaper be right there beside you just when you not figurin' him at all. 'Course, he might be real cool to you, smile a lot. He gots a wide smile. Why not? He be totally stoked with his job. Nobody put *him* out of work."

Robby snagged his board from the gravel. "Aw, quit tryin' to scare me with werewolf talk, man. Jeez, no wonder Slimer's a crazy-boy, hangin' with you. Hey, it's like you know what you're sayin', but it only sounds weird when anybody else talks that way."

Eric shrugged again. "I not be tryin' to scare you, raisin-boy, just be tellin' you what is. Teach you lessons like in school. Just 'cause Rats an' Animals gettin' friendly now, maybe sharin' the Uzis, don't mean these night streets be total safe for kids." He smiled. " 'Sides, you not be scared of me anyways. You be too smart. Maybe not even believe in werewolves, huh?"

Robby smiled. "I don't know why everybody keeps callin' me smart, man. Maybe sometime I'll figure out what it means." He yawned. "So? What's up, wolf-boy?"

"Moon, stars, us."

"Yeah? Well, not me for long. I gotta get over to Donny's. Jeez, ain't you cold up there without no shirt?" Robby grinned. "Oh yeah, I forgot, werewolves don't get cold or somethin'. Um, ain't seen you in awhile. Donny says you ain't in school this year. You drop out totally?"

Eric gazed up at the roofs. "Figure I learn all what that school can tell me." He turned and studied Robby. "You should be goin', man. You smart enough to know the dogshit from the good stuff."

"Yeah? So maybe I'll get smart enough to make chump-change in Burger King, right?"

Eric shook his head. "Things you need to know be in school too. An' they free. You say I smart? Okay, raisin-boy, listen. Use your mind, don't cost nuthin' an' nobody can take it away from you, 'less you get into drugs an' lose it your ownself. Know what? You be a dude what gots a chance of gettin' outa this dogshit, *for*-ever."

"So, what about you?"

Eric smiled. "Werewolves like King Kong, do what they fuckin' well want in this universe. Leastways, till somebody come along with a silver bullet."

"Well, me an' Donny been kinda talkin' about that. Like, maybe I could try sneakin' into class with him or another Animal. Donny says that school's got so many kids anyhow that maybe the teachers never even know I ain't on paper. Be kinda hot, goin' to school for no reason other than you wanted to, huh?"

"I like your mind, dude."

"Um, so what'er you doin' in Animal-land tonight anyways?"

Eric showed teeth. "I need permission?"

" 'Course not. Anyhow, who'd fuck with you? Um, you talkin' to dead kids?"

"Not tonight. It be a peaceful night. Ghosts all restin', polishin' their bones."

"Even T.C.?"

Eric showed teeth again, and for just a second it was scary. "What I tell you, man? Forget T.C.!"

"It's hard."

"Mmm. That 'cause you a good dude."

"Um, don't it make you sad, knowing all about death an' stuff? Like, Slimer keeps sayin' you can look in some dude's eyes an' know if he's gonna die soon. I think that'd make me sad."

Eric smiled a little. "Slimer be a crazy boy, remember? You shouldn't be listenin' to shit he say." He grinned. "Maybe he really be hangin' with me too much?" His grin faded. " 'Sides, what is, is. Tell you a wolf secret. Some kids gotta be sad for others to be happy. Universe a funny place that way, need balance sorta. We live in dogshit so others can be squids. I still not figure why, but it got to be like that. Why there be so much hurt for some an' showtime for others? That's what *I* got to learn now, Robby, not the rest of that school dogshit." He smiled once more. "You a happy dude, inside. Maybe I be sad so you can be happy. That's okay."

Robby sighed and looked at the sky. "I don't understand stuff like that, man."

"You want to be a werewolf?"

"I don't think so."

"Then, that stuff not be important for you. Two-an'-two stuff be important. Readin' books what don't got no pictures be important. You come over to Rat-land anytime. I give you permanent permission. I read you stuff, then make you read stuff. Same as skatin', gotta practice with your mind to get good."

"Books with no pictures are hard, man."

Eric tapped his forehead. "You gotta make the pictures in here."

Robby thought awhile, looking back at the soft black above. "What's it like, bein' a werewolf?"

"Cold."

Robby giggled. "Too funny." He dug a Marlboro pack from his pocket and shook out two cigarettes. Eric made a match come out of nowhere and fired them.

"That's hot," said Robby. "Um, would you teach me stuff like that too, or is it only for werewolves?"

"You read one of my books got no pictures, I teach you that."

Robby studied Eric a moment. "You didn't mean 'cold' cold, huh?"

Smoke trickled from Eric's nose. "No."

"Um, what's death, man?"

"Cold."

"Don't give me werewolf talk! Say what I ask." Robby met Eric's eyes.

"You held T.C.'s hand. You don't need to ask."

"But, where is he now?"

Robby'd seen black ice on the Fresno streets and that's what Eric's eyes were. Eric hissed out smoke. "I say one last time T.C. restin' awhile. He not evil like Squeaker, never made that choice. Maybe he get another chance. Maybe get to be a regular kid. That all you need to know."

"But—"

Eric moved suddenly, grabbing Robby's shoulders and shaking him hard. "Hear me, asshole! You want to help T.C.?"

" 'Course!"

"Then forget him!" Eric held Robby's shoulders tight. "Maybe you don't even know it, man, but you're wishin' him back. Yes you are! Long's you keep doin' that, he never never get outa this dogshit place. You keepin' him chained here like total slavers. Worse, man, pretty soon he stop even tryin' to leave an' become part of you! Then neither one of you ever get away. Now, you understand?"

"What if . . . what if I was dead too?"

"T.C. never learned to skate."

"What?"

Eric took his hands away and smiled his funny V smile. "You wanna cruise the universe with some dude you don't even know?"

Robby started to laugh. "You are weird, man. Hey, maybe I could teach him."

Eric grinned. "This not be talk for happy raisin-boys. You not worry over Mr. Death. He gonna leave you alone a long, long time."

For a moment Robby seemed satisfied. Then his eyes clouded again. "Yeah. How long, man? Long enough so it's worth it to learn to read book with no pictures? Check my eyes. Tell me how long."

Eric frowned. "Now *you* not funny, dude. It not be cool to mess with that shit. Mr. Reaper ain't no showtime."

"Aw, shit. You just said I was gonna live awhile, like it's in the plan or somethin'."

Eric blew smoke and shook his head. "You not listenin' to me, dude. Only the squids think there be some kind of plan. Like a lifetime guarantee. Death do what he fuckin' well want, change his mind any old time, even play a joke. Figure. There be a zillion kids, man. Keep Mr. Reaper total busy. Maybe he just not got time for you right now. But don't be tuggin' at his robe, man. Don't be tellin' him, hey, check me out." Eric sighed and looked down at the sidewalk. "Sometimes I wonder if that's what I do when I look in somebody's eyes. Like sayin', hey, Mr. D., check out this dude." He looked up and smiled. "See, I still be learnin' this werewolf stuff. Not totally got it down yet."

Robby took a hit off his cigarette and nodded. "I think I hear you." He thought a minute. "But, wouldn't that mean, like you kill the kids? Slimer told me about that time in school when the big dude tried homo stuff with you."

Eric's face saddened in the glow of his Marlboro. "I sorry I done that now. It be total wrong. He wasn't a bad dude, just confused a little like most kids be. Didn't deserve death. That makes me sad, to kill not knowin'." He made a box with his long fingers. "This I know for sure. Things all be connected in some mega way. What happens here, make a thing happen there. But, maybe, not always. Somebody hurt me, they really just hurtin' themselves, only by the time it come back around to 'em they probably forgot what they done to deserve it." He spread his hands. "That what wrong with this whole place, man. Squids hurtin' us, but by universe law, they really hurtin' their ownselves. Only, they don't believe, so all this hurtin' just keep goin' in a huge circle. No wonder nobody happy, even when they got all kinds of cool stuff. But, maybe when I looked in that dude's eyes, I made his circle real small. Made Death notice him. Death had a little free time, say to himself, hmmm, why not?"

Robby's eyes widened a little and he stepped back. "Oh, jeez. For sure I wouldn't never want you pissed at me. Suppose you thought somethin' bad about somebody just by accident? No wonder everybody's scared of you."

Eric turned away. "So now you be scared too?"

Robby reached out slowly and touched Eric's arm. "Cold means lonely, huh?"

"Sometimes." Eric faced Robby and took his shoulders gently. "Come stay with me tonight, Robby."

Robby felt Eric's warm hands and his body tensed. Eric let him go and smiled sadly. "Yeah, you be scared of me now too."

Robby jammed his hands in his pockets, spit out his cigarette and stomped it. The fog breathed cold around him and he shivered. When he spoke his voice was husky. "It's not that, man. Really. You, um, scare me in a different way more." He dropped his eyes to the sidewalk. "It's like, just now, bein' close to you, touchin' you, makes me feel like a homo or somethin'. Like when Slimer brought me to see you. I wanted to touch you then . . . " He looked up and his eyes hardened. "Goddammit, you make me all confused."

Eric shrugged, studying the ruby point of his cigarette. "Like Slimer tell you that day. It just my aura or somethin'. You be no homo. Every dude think stuff like that."

Robby put a foot on his board and rolled it back and forth. "I don't know what to believe anymore. Everybody lies."

Eric flipped his cigarette into the gutter. "Do the Animals lie?"

" 'Course not. That ain't what I meant." Robby waved around at the dark silent buildings. "The world lies, man. 'Specially to kids."

Eric smiled. "For sure the world lies. But the universe don't." He thumped his chest. "You got the whole universe right in here, man. Anytime you get confused, just make your mind all quiet and listen to what it say. Maybe hard to quiet your head when people shootin' at you, shovin' crackers in your face, chasin' you down a alley. That stuff be mega huge to a kid, but only chump-change to the universe. Maybe sound like TV, but you get whatever you really want if you want it bad enough."

Robby spat. "Did T.C. want to die, man?"

"Was T.C. listenin' to his heart when he was shootin' at you?"

Robby's head snapped up and his eyes narrowed. "Yeah? Now I *know* you're talkin' dogshit, man. A dude I knew back in Fresno was just skatin' down the street one day an' some drive-by fuckers just killed him, no reason at all. Was he listenin' to his heart, asshole? He never hurt nobody in his life!"

Surprisingly, Eric laughed. "That's like sayin', long's you're a good dude you can't get run over by a truck or part of a buildin' couldn't fall on you, huh? Maybe Death be the baddest dude in the world, man, but he only work for the universe, like a janitor. We all here to do jobs, man, an' most times I figure our jobs be to stay cool an' help others do their jobs the best we can."

"Aw, that's dogshit, man. Like church stuff. Like, you're supposed to hurt like hell so's you can go to heaven or somethin', right? I don't think I believe there's anythin' after this at all."

155

"So why you carryin' T.C. around with you?"

Robby shook his head. "You're right, man. I never want to be a werewolf. I could never understand all that stuff. What's the use of bein' good if shit can still happen to you anyways?"

"Maybe only that bein' good makes you happy inside an' being bad don't. Think about it."

Robby sighed and looked at Eric a long time. "I gotta book, man," he said finally. "It's gettin' late. Maybe you're right, maybe you're just full of shit. Maybe I'll think about it." Robby smiled a little. "Later, Eric. Maybe I'll come over tomorrow."

Eric's teeth flashed. "Anytime, Robby." He spun around and darted into the fog, big Cons silent.

Robby gazed after him awhile, then decked and rolled. It felt good with the cold grayness rushing past. He jumped the gutter, catching air, cut the street, and slammed the curb. The crack of his board against concrete echoed like a shot between the old brick buildings. He snapped the nose down and ripped on, thinking of Donny now. They could talk awhile under the warm blanket before going to sleep. Maybe he'd even try sneaking into school tomorrow.

"Yo! Shredder-bro."

The voice was friendly and somehow familiar. Robby saw the van's dark shape and smelled the hot engine as he tailed. He remembered now, the white kid with the steel teeth from that first night. The van was parked on the wrong side of the street near an alley mouth.

"Wanna smoke, brother?"

Robby hesitated, trying to recall his feelings from that lonely sunset time. Maybe the dude would've taken him to the real ocean. Things could've been better. But, then he'd of never met the Animals. Or Squeaker. Robby flipped up his board and came slowly over to the driver's window, ready to book fast. But the white boy only smiled, teeth glinting in the streetlight glow. "What's up?" the dude asked, holding out a Camel Filters pack.

Robby took one, and the dude fired a Bic. Robby sucked smoke and shrugged. "Just skatin' home again, man." It felt different now to say that, because in a way, he was.

The dude seemed to study him a moment and his blue eyes nar-

156

rowed a little. Then he grinned. "For sure. I remember you now." He snickered. "You live by the ocean, right?"

Robby considered. "Yeah. I do."

The dude snickered again. "Ain't much of an ocean, y'know?"

"It's enough."

The dude look puzzled for an instant, then smiled. "School tomorrow, huh? That sucks. Um, what kinda skate?"

"The same. Steadham."

"Yeah?" said another voice in the van. "I used to have one of them. Hot skate, man."

Robby looked in. There was a black kid about the same age as the driver. He had a short black-punk haircut, a huge earring, and wore only a sleeveless Levi jacket over his muscled chest. Chains rustled as he leaned over to give Robby a grin. There was a look in his eyes that Robby'd only seen a few times in his life. It was hard to describe, but kind of like, hey, I'm black, too, see? Robby wasn't sure why, but it bothered him.

"I'm Jody," said the driver-kid. "This's my homey, Alvin."

Robby thought of the Chipmunks and smiled a little. Who was scared of chipmunks?

"Robby," said Robby.

Jody snickered once more. "No street name, brother?"

Robby glanced across at Alvin. "All of us don't got street names, man."

Jody looked like he thought he'd missed something, but didn't know what it was. He grinned. "Hey, Robby. You into scorin' a half-buck?"

"Aw, it's kinda late, man."

"Hey, this's easy, bro. Watcher. Only takes a little while. Still get lots of sleep for motherfuckin' school."

Robby almost smiled again. That word sounded so lame when Jody said it. Still, he considered, spinning a wheel on his board. Kevin had found a set of used Kryponics at a skate shop. They wanted ten dollars for them. There was a lot of hot stuff he could do with a whole half-buck. He came close. "Yeah? Where?"

Jody pointed to the alley. "Right here. Be somebody along . . . " —

he glanced at the three watches on his wrist—". . . anytime. All you gotta do is keep the street clean a few minutes."

Robby wondered a moment if this was something Randers would like him doing. Then he remembered what Eric had said and tried to make his mind quiet.

Engine sound came faint from the next block, quiet rumble of glass-packs.

Jody grinned again. "Right on!" He held a fifty out to Robby. "Hey, bro, up front even. C'mon, it's only business."

Robby glanced up the street. Then he nodded and took the bill. Jody reached out and shook his hand in the old kid-shake that they still did in Fresno. "Awesome, Robby. Be cool now."

Jody fired the van's engine as a thrashed old 'Stang cruised from the fog and slowed. The driver, a chubby white squidy-looking boy about Jody's age, leaned out of the window. Jody pointed to the alley and the white kid nodded and swung the car in. Robby saw another white boy beside him, thinner, maybe younger.

Jody left his lights off, pulled up, then reversed into the alley. Robby rolled to the wall and stood by a corner, smoking. The alley was a dead-ender, he knew. The dude in the 'Stang couldn't have been doing this kind of stuff very long or he'd of backed in too. Robby shrugged, not his prob. Both engines cut and he smiled, blowing smoke, feeling the bill in his pocket. This kind of thing never took long. Maybe Eric was right about things being connected? After all, if Eric hadn't been there, he'd already be at Donny's and missed this deal.

Robby watched the empty street, both ways, and listened hard. This was really an easy job but he might as well do it right. Jody was a totally careful dude, smart, too. Probably only sixteen, but already had his own van, and able to pay a whole half-buck for a few minutes watching. You *had* to be smart to get in a place like that. Robby frowned a little. Drugs, for sure, probably crack. But Jody and Alvin definitely weren't from around here, so the crack was going out of Oakland. That had to be all right. How could Randers get pissed off about that?

Robby breathed smoke and thought. For sure he'd share this money with the Animals. They all knew he needed the wheels, but Kevin needed a new deck. Randers would decide in the end, but Robby was sure he'd get the wheels.

In the darkness behind, there were low voices, the click of a trunk lid, and the soft rolling of the van's side door. Springs squeaked as stuff was loaded. After, there were more muffled words, then silence. Finally, Jody's voice called soft, "Yo, Robby?"

Robby turned. "Yeah?"

"Everything cool?"

"Totally. Nuthin' movin' for blocks, man."

"Yeah? All right. Come an' have a beer, bro. Help you sleep better for school."

"Well, it's really kinda late, man."

"Hey, that's okay," Jody snickered. "You can take it with you."

Robby considered. He really was tired. But Jody sounded so friendly and cool, like he didn't care if Robby was younger or not. And he hadn't lied back when he'd said he had a black friend. Robby flipped his cigarette away and walked into the alley.

The van had its parking lights on now, amber eyes in front, ruby glow to the rear, lighting the back of the 'Stang. Robby saw the two white boys standing by the open trunk. The chubby kid's shirt was too small and his belly hung out a little, making him look even younger. The light was too dim to make out their faces, but the chubby one seemed to flick his eyes at Robby and shake his head quick.

Robby stopped. Fear had a smell, and it came thick from the foggy darkness. He tensed and spun around, but Alvin stepped out from behind a dumpster. His grin was friendly, but he held a Mac Ten.

"Go with the other dudes, little shredder," he said.

"Shit," said Robby. It sounded stupid as hell, but what else was there to say? He felt sweat all over his body and smelled his own fear as he walked around the side of the van and into the ruddy glow.

He saw that the white boys were probably about fifteen and sixteen. The chubby kid's shirt had an old Alva skate graphic on the front. It was the hot one that you couldn't get anymore; no wonder he still wore it. The boy gave Robby a strange sad glance. Robby'd never seen that look on a white face before. Then the boy gazed back away into nothing. The other kid was shaking and tears glistened on his cheeks.

He just stared down at the pavement and seemed to be choking back sobs.

Jody stood behind the van, one big Nike on the bumper. He gave Robby another friendly metal-grin and waved him between the white kids with the muzzle of his Ten. Robby couldn't think. It was like the night they'd killed Squeaker, like nothing was real anymore. His throat tightened and the words came out funny. "But, I'm only a kid."

Jody cocked his head a moment, then smiled and nodded. "I know, brother. So am I." He held out his hand and Robby was confused. Jody grinned again. "The money, Robby. Otherwise it'll get all messy."

Robby's hand shook as he dug out the bill and gave it to Jody. The gun muzzle waved again, and Robby pressed back between the bigger boys. The thin one started to cry like a little kid, not caring anymore. Robby took the boy's hand. It was chill, but the fingers curled tight over Robby's.

Alvin moved beside Jody.

Jody leaned forward a little and smiled at Robby once more. "Hey, don't cry, Robby. This's nothin' personal. You could've been any kid." He held up his hand the way Spock did on Star Trek. "The Force be with you."

Both Tens fired.

Eric was sitting on a roof, his back against warm chimney brick, when he heard the auto-fire. He was up and running toward it warp-speed, but it cut off before he reached the next building. He was across the other roof and scrambling to the third when the Mopar started and tires screamed. He slipped on fog-slicked tarpaper, but was up and running again when the sound of a car skidding carried down the block. Engine thunder echoed in the street, fading into the distant rumble of 880 traffic as he leaped to the last roof and headed for the black gap of alleyway. He jerked out the .22, cocking it as he ran and hoping the safety would hold this time.

He suddenly smelled blood and slammed to a stop by a fire ladder, staring down into darkness, nostrils flaring. Exhaust fumes drifted up, their oiliness mixed with nose-burning tire smoke, gunpowder, and lots of blood. He crouched, peering over the edge, noting the 'Stang's dim shape, scenting its hot steel. He waited, listened, holding his breath, trying to quiet his heart. There was nothing but the slow regular tink of an engine cooling off. He felt the night-cold and shivered, but still waited. No voices, no distant approaching sirens, only a fog-muffled diesel on the freeway. He counted three more tinks from the engine below then stuck the gun in his teeth and swung down the ladder.

The last section was folded up, but he dropped the ten feet to trash-strewn concrete and crouched beside a dumpster. The engine ticked twice more, slower now. Eric eased toward the car, gun up and ready in both hands like the cops did. Blood-smell washed over him like fog swirls, coppery like new pennies, and his mouth went salty. There were fainter scents and he sorted them—piss-wet jeans, older kid sweat . . . and another.

"No!" he whispered. "Please."

He lowered his gun and took a breath, then moved around the back of the car, already knowing what he'd see. There were Robby's black glistening curls between the blond tangles of the older boys. Eric crouched and listened. No breathing, nothing. He knew there wouldn't be, yet a warmth lingered over the three still forms and drew him closer. He automatically made a match come from nowhere, eyes slitted against the yellow glare, looking once at the kids and then no more. The match flickered and died. That wasn't Robby's face any longer, not the face he wanted to remember. Eric felt his heart trying to pull Robby back, but that wasn't right. Eric squeezed his eyes tight shut and forced himself to let go. "Book," he whispered, "book to the light, dude."

He moved away and glanced around. Still no sound in the streets. Nobody even called the cops about shooting anymore.

Eric had a stupid idea, a kid's stupid idea. Get the Animals to come and take Robby away. Have a kid-funeral, a ceremony. Why let the old people have him now? They didn't give a shit about him when he was alive. Stupid idea, something like Slimer would say.

Tears filled Eric's eyes. Werewolves weren't supposed to cry. Neither were Animals, but Eric knew they would. Maybe that was

161

ceremony enough. Street kids didn't waste tears. Robby's board lay nearby. Its wheels were in the air. Like some kind of fucking joke.

Eric snagged it. Kevin needed a new board. Gun in one hand, skateboard in the other, Eric walked into the street.